CIRCUS OF THIEVES

SIMON AND SCHUSTER
London New York Sydney Toronto New Delhi

CIRCUS OF THIEVES

AND THE RAFFLE OF DOOM

WILLIAM SUTCLIFFE

ILLUSTRATED BY DAVID TAZZYMAN

First published in Great Britain in 2014 by Simon and Schuster UK Ltd
1st Floor, 222 Gray's Inn Road, London, WC1X 8HB
A CBS COMPANY

Text copyright © 2014 William Sutcliffe
Illustrations copyright © 2014 David Tazzyman

HB 978-1-4711-2255-2
PB 978-1-4711-2023-7
eBook ISBN 978-1-4711-2024-4
1 3 5 7 9 10 8 6 4 2

This book is a work of fiction. Any resemblance to actual people living
or dead, events or locales is entirely coincidental.

Printed and bound by CPI Group (UK) Ltd, Croydon, CR0 4YY

www.simonandschuster.co.uk
www.simonandschuster.com.au

For Saul, Iris and Juno,
with love and gratitude – WS

To my Awesome Mel x – DT

ONE

A boy on a camel

IT STARTED WITH A RUMBLE and a clatter and a faint trembling of the air. At first, only the animals noticed.

Fluffypants McBain, the tabby cat from the Post Office, moved one ear towards the noise, thought for a second, and having established that the sound did not indicate the arrival of food, went back to sleep. Magnificat, the far-too-pleased-with-himself Bengal from the pub, who had stolen all of Fluffypants' territory except for half a windowsill, turned his head towards the unusual noise and immediately calculated that it was being made by a large group of humans travelling in unusually shaped vehicles. The real puzzle was a faint clip-clopping, to the rhythm of hooves, but without the hardness of a horse or a cow. This was something else. Something loping and tall. Magnificat raised his tail in a look-how-beautiful-I-am way and looked around, to see if anyone else had noticed or interpreted the sounds wafting into town.

Of course they hadn't. It really was tedious to live in a place where everyone else was so much less intelligent (not to mention less beautiful) than oneself.

He yawned and stretched – for a second feeling the urge for a doze, a meal, a cuddle and a fight, all at once – then prowled on down the high street, in search of something else to do. This large, mysteriously-hooved creature, he decided, was probably best avoided.

Fizzer was the next to notice. Fizzer ought to have been an astronomer or a nuclear physicist or at the very least a university professor, but unfortunately these career paths hadn't opened up to him, so he had to settle for being a dog. He knew something big and important was arriving, and he suspected it might change the whole town forever, but at this moment there were several trees on his morning walk that he'd not yet sniffed, and this vital task simply had to be finished before he could set about researching the identity of the intruders. It's amazing what you can find out from sniffing a tree, specially if you happen to be Fizzer. He considered himself to be the town's unofficial police dog, and the trees of the high street were his private CCTV network. Just half an hour of careful sniffing, and Fizzer knew exactly who had been where and when (and what they'd eaten for breakfast).

Hannah was the first human to notice that

something was up. She was busy doing an experiment with flying fish (not real ones, paper ones) to see whether big ones or small ones fly furthest when you drop them out of your bedroom window,☺ when she felt the trembling of the air and heard the clatter and rumble that had twitched Fluffypants' ear, raised Magnificat's tail and diverted Fizzer from his tree sniffing. Hannah, being just a human, didn't have any idea what this sound might indicate, but being a human in possession of an unusually perceptive and curious brain, she knew it was her task to find out. She also knew this job was urgent, far too urgent to leave time for such boring things as breakfast and getting dressed.

She ran downstairs in her pyjamas, jumped into a pair of wellies, shouted to her Mum something along the lines of, 'Mumble mumble mumble shop mumble mumble BACK SOON BYEEE!' and darted out of the front door.

☺Answer: small ones.

Almost immediately, she passed Fizzer, who looked up from a particularly rich and fascinating tree trunk, noticed Hannah's speed and unusual outfit, and gave her a quizzical but knowing look which seemed to say, "Are you going to check out that noise?"

She paused and scratched him between the ears,🐕 a gesture which Fizzer took to mean, 'Yes. Do you want to come, or are you too busy reading your pee-mails?'

🐕 Note to non-dog people: this is friendly. Dogs like it. Note to non-human people: humans don't like it. Scratching humans between the ears is not considered friendly and shouldn't be attempted without asking permission first.

Fizzer raised his head, reluctantly withdrawing his nostrils from the quite exquisite odour left by Princess (the precious, prancing, primped poodle who presided over her prized pack of panicky puppies in a palatial parlour on Privet Place) and shook his bottom, which in Fizzer's language meant, 'Why not?' or, more specifically, 'I wasn't going to bother, but I like a spot of company, so let's go.'

They headed off together, along the high street, through the rows of small red-brick houses that circled the town, then out into open fields, with Hannah running as fast as she could and Fizzer

walking as slowly as he was able without feeling like he was going backwards.

Fizzer often felt sorry for humans. It must be incredibly frustrating to have to do everything *so slowly*, and to be practically blind, nose-wise, not to mention half deaf and totally ignorant about everything of any real importance. If it wasn't for their ability to open tins of dog food, humans would be almost completely useless. He liked Hannah, though. She was much less dumb than the rest of them.

Just past the level crossing, Hannah and Fizzer saw something that made them stop dead, almost as if they had both crashed into an invisible glass wall. Weaving down a narrow, rutted road that was normally only used by tractors, rabbits and lost hikers was the strangest and most extraordinary procession of vehicles and animals either of them had ever come across.

At the front was a camel. On top of the camel was a boy dressed from head to toe in purple velvet, singing at the top of his voice. Behind the camel was an elephant, which was being ridden by a man who was lying on his back, fast asleep. Behind that was a camper van with two deck chairs on the roof, containing a man in a leotard who seemed to be waxing his moustache, and a woman wearing what was either three thimbles tied together with string, or a very skimpy bikini. The camper van was towing a caravan, which was towing another caravan, which was towing another caravan. It was, you could say, a caravan of caravans. Behind that was a huge articulated lorry,🚌 painted with rainbows and butterflies and flowers and ice cream and smiley faces and shooting stars and dancing puppies. Emblazoned on the side in chunky 3D letters were the words **SHANK'S IMPOSSIBLE CIRCUS.**

'It's the circus!' cried Hannah.

'*Муиии,*' replied Fizzer, sarcastically, meaning, 'Thanks for explaining.'

Hannah spun round on the heel of her wellies and began to run back towards town, shouting, 'It's the circus! It's the circus! It's the circus!'

Fizzer stayed put, knowing she was about to change her mind.

Hannah stopped. An amazing, incredible thought had just popped into her brain. The camel! The boy! One camel, one boy, *two* humps. She could ask for a lift! OK, so the pyjama and welly combo wasn't exactly ideal for hitchhiking, but the boy

---

🚌 This does not mean a lorry that talks posh. That would be an articulate lorry, which is another matter altogether. An articulated lorry is one that bends in the middle, which has no bearing on the vehicle's verbal skills. All humans bend in the middle, as you probably know, yet some are far more articulate than others. Penguins do not bend in the middle, and are also strikingly inarticulate, but their lack of bendiness is probably not to blame.

was basically dressed in a pair of curtains, so she didn't think he'd be too bothered. And as for the rest of the town, who on earth would notice your clothes when you were riding a camel?

She turned and ran back to tell Fizzer about her fantastic idea, but saw immediately in his eyes and the tilt of his head that he'd figured it all out already. Hannah didn't like feeling patronised by a dog so, as they stood and waited for the camel, she decided to make up a fact designed to impress him.

'Circuses are famous for picking up hitch-hikers,' she said in a school-teachery voice. 'It's an ancient custom of the circus community.'

Fizzer raised one eyebrow. He was unconvinced.

'It's true,' said Hannah. 'I read a book about it.'

Fizzer lowered the other eyebrow. It was almost impossible to impress Fizzer with anything, least of all with made-up facts, which his encyclopaedically intelligent nose seemed to sniff out with unerring accuracy.

'Here's the camel!' said Hannah, who had realised it was time to change the subject.

As the procession approached, three things became clear. First, that the boy's song was about an ant from Antarctica, a cat from Catalonia and a phoenix from Phoenix; second, that his singing voice was so loud and out-of-tune and lacking in any sense of rhythm that it was enough to make nearby plants wilt in horror; and third, that despite the plant-wilting tunelessness of his melody, this boy sang with all the joy and gusto of an operatic maestro performing to a thousand adoring fans. As a result, there was something weirdly, uglily ♪ beautiful about it.

Only when the boy was directly in front of Hannah and Fizzer did he stop singing, much to the relief of the local plant life, which quickly

---

♫ Uglily isn't a word. You know that. I know that. Let's just move on.

pinged back upwards towards the sun.

'Ho, there!' he said to his camel, pulling the reins, halting his big beige bulbous beast. The boy looked Hannah up and down slowly, starting with her wellies and working his eyes upwards. 'Nice pyjamas,' he said, eventually.

'Thanks,' replied Hannah. 'Nice camel.'

'He's called Narcissus,' said the boy. 'And if I made a list of a hundred words to describe him, I reckon "nice" would be at the bottom.'

Narcissus raised his droopy lips, showing a murky keyboard of long yellow teeth, and spat out a blob of camel goo which landed with a splat on Hannah's left welly.

'See?' said the boy. 'But that doesn't mean I don't love him. Why be nice when you can be a camel?' He patted its hairy neck and the camel farted appreciatively. At that moment, like a strange echo, the enormous lorry let out an enormous honk.

'That's my dad,' said the boy. 'Driving that lorry turns him into a total . . . oop.' The lorry's second honk drowned out a mysterious cluster of syllables, but it was pretty clear to Hannah that the boy wasn't complimenting his dad's driving.

'Do you want a lift?' the boy asked.

'Yes, please,' said Hannah. 'How do I get on?'

'Willpower, strength and good luck,' he replied, from his high perch.

'Oh, I've got all of those,' said Hannah. 'Watch this.'

With that, she turned, ran a few steps, climbed the nearest tree and edged along a branch that overhung the road. 'You step forward, I'll jump on,' she instructed.

'That's not how we usually do it,' the boy said, hesitantly, 'but I'll try anything once.'

Fizzer raised one eyebrow again and stepped back, away from the fall-out zone.

Narcissus yawned as Billy edged him into position. It took a lot to surprise Narcissus. A girl dressed in pyjamas and wellies was about to jump out of a tree and use him as a landing mat – so what? Even if this was the most ill-advised, badly-planned and likeliest-to-end-in-injury attempt to mount a camel that he had ever encountered – big deal.

While Hannah prepared herself for the jump, Narcissus drifted off again, back to his favourite daydream, which was, as always, about taramasalata.

'Ready?' said Hannah. '3 . . . 2 . . . 1 . . .'

The exact thing Hannah wanted to be more than anything else in the world

THE MANOEUVRE didn't exactly go to plan, what with Hannah landing backwards on top of the boy's head, flattening him and wedging his face into a camel hump with her bum on his right ear. As Hannah tried to squirm herself into position, she heard a muffled voice say, 'The thing you're sitting on isn't a saddle. It's my head.'

Eventually, she got herself up onto the rear hump and the boy, looking only slightly squashed-faced, congratulated her on her inventiveness.

'Thanks,' she replied. 'Sorry I sat on you.'

'That's OK. Hold on tight,' he said, advice which wasn't strictly necessary, since riding this animal was like sitting on a seesaw strapped to a supermarket trolley rolling around the deck of a boat on a stormy day in the middle of the Atlantic.

'Just feel the motion with your legs, and go with it,' said the boy, whose body swayed gently from side to side, while Hannah's flipped and flopped

and lurched and jounced, like a puppet in a washing machine.

'You getting the hang of it?'

'Oh, yeah. No sweat,' said Hannah, relieved that he was staring calmly ahead, rather than looking back at her, in which case he might have noticed that she was now upside down, doing the splits, clinging on to a lump of camel hair for dear life, with her legs in the air and her nose in a far smellier part of the camel than any sane person would normally approach without a face mask.

'Fun, isn't it?' he said.

'Yeah. Great.'

Without turning round, the boy reached backwards, grabbed one of Hannah's ankles, and gave her leg a flick which sent her body spinning upwards, back onto the rear hump.

'I'd work on your stunt moves later if I were you,' he said.

'Good idea,' Hannah replied, enjoying the feeling of right-way-upness, a delicious sensation which she now realised was far too often taken for granted.

'I'm Billy,' said the boy. 'Billy Shank. Junior member of Shank's Impossible Circus, heir to the Shank Entertainment Empire.'

'I'm Hannah,' said Hannah. 'Like Anna, but hiding between two "H"s.'

'I like you,' said Billy.

'Oh,' said Hannah.

For a moment she couldn't think how to reply to this strange comment, and she knew 'Oh' was not a sufficient response. Then she heard herself say, 'I like you, too.'

Only as these words came out of her mouth did she realise this was a perfect description of how she felt. It seemed odd to say this kind of thing out loud when you've only known someone for a few minutes, but also kind of exciting, like finding a good short cut, or skipping the main course and going straight to dessert. Using somebody's head as a camel saddle, she reflected, was clearly a quick way to form a friendship.♥

'Narcissus is a good judge of character, and he thinks you're OK, so you must be,' said Billy.

'How can you tell he thinks I'm OK?'

'Because he only spat on your wellies. If he didn't like you it wouldn't have been your wellies. That's about as affectionate as he gets.'

'Wow. I'm flattered.'

'You're not a wimp like all the others.'

'All what others?'

'Civilians.'

'Who?'

'Civilians. People who aren't in the circus.'

'Oh. I see,' replied Hannah, feeling a rush of pride tingle in her chest at Billy's assessment of her

---

♥Take note. You may find this information useful in later life. On the other hand, you may not.

character. 'Not a wimp' was the exact thing Hannah wanted to be more than anything else in the world.

'I think Fizzer likes *you*,' said Hannah, more out of a desire to return his friendliness than from any real evidence.

'I know,' said Billy.

'How do you know?' said Hannah, slightly affronted.

'Because it's obvious.'

Hannah looked down at Fizzer, who was trotting companionably alongside Narcissus. He looked back up at her and said, '*Nyumnyapupupu*,' with a subtle but definite nod. There was no doubting that this meant, 'He's right. I like him.'

Now Hannah was really impressed. 🐕

'Are you going to come tonight?' asked Billy.

'Where?'

'To the show. We'll be on this evening.'

'Er . . . I hope so. I mean, I'd love to, but I didn't

🐕 'Who is Fizzer?' I hear you ask. 'Is he Hannah's dog? Or somebody else's? How did he get to be so preposterously clever? Is he working for the government?' Patience, my friends, patience. All will be revealed. Probably.

know anything about it.'

'Nobody knows. We never announce our shows in advance.'

'Why not?'

'That's not our style.'

'But wouldn't it be better if people knew you were coming?'

'It would be a disaster.'

'How could that be a disaster?'

'Nobody can know where we are.'

'Nobody?'

'Nobody official.'

'Official? What does that mean? Who's official? Am I official?'

'*Are you?*' Billy span round to face Hannah and eyeballed her fiercely.

'Am I what?'

'Official.'

'I don't know. What's official?'

'Police.'

'Police!?' shrieked Hannah.

'SHHHHH!'

Hannah lowered her voice. 'Of course I'm not police. I'm a child.'

'Hmm,' said Billy. 'I suppose you are.'

'What are you talking about?'

Billy leaned towards Hannah and whispered, 'Don't tell anyone I told you this, but we're on the run.'

'From who?'

'Everyone.'

'Are you serious?'

Billy shifted on the hump, his rump taking a bump from the jump and pump of the lump. 'Sort of.'

'What do you mean?'

'Oh, nothing! I'm only joking. Just messing about. Winding you up.' Billy slapped himself on the thigh, like a dodgy panto actor, let out an unconvincing laugh, and turned back to face the road.

Hannah, who was good at sensing the subtle meanings that sometimes sneak out between the words people actually speak, detected something strange in Billy's tone of voice. She had an odd feeling that just as air pushes against the sides of a balloon that's about to pop, Billy was struggling to hold in something important. His sort-of joke felt like a tiny leak of a secret that wanted to burst out of him. Hannah decided to take what is often a wise course of action when the person you're talking to isn't being entirely honest: she said nothing.

'You shouldn't take everything so seriously,' said Billy, who happened to be good at sensing the subtle meanings that can be expressed by a few seconds of silence. He knew that Hannah suspected the true meaning behind his sort-of joke. Billy had never told any civilian about the secret of Shank's Impossible Circus, and now, after knowing her for only a few minutes, he had already almost let it slip to Hannah, but he was surprised to find that he didn't care.

He'd never befriended a civilian before. It was a strange, exciting and slightly dizzy-making feeling.

'So how do you get an audience if you never announce the show?' Hannah asked.

'You'll see.'

'Will I?'

'Yup. Just keep your eyes and ears open, and if you hear anything that sounds like applause, follow the noise. But if you see me, and I look like I'm working, don't come and speak to me.'

'OK.'

'And when I am working, it may look as if I'm not working, but I probably am. Do you understand?'

'Yes,' said Hannah, though if she was being honest she would have said something more along the lines of, 'No.'

'I'm just saying I'll find you. Don't you find me.'

'Are you trying extra hard to be mysterious, or does it come naturally?' she asked.

'Oh, I practise in the mirror every morning. Do you want to see my mysterious face?'

'OK.'

'I have several, but I think this is the best one.'

Billy swivelled on his hump to face her so he was now riding backwards. His mouth was half open, one eye was shut and his nostrils were flaring in and out. Hannah told him he looked like he was being attacked by a jellyfish, and he let out a big, throaty laugh. Or, rather, he let out half a big, throaty laugh, because in the middle of it he suddenly stopped and a look of terror overtook his face. This wasn't fake terror, either. This was the real thing.

Billy stared behind Hannah, his eyes wide and his mouth clamped shut.

Hannah turned to see what had changed his mood so suddenly, and was immediately blinded by the headlights of the enormous lorry. These weren't just ordinary lights, the kind that sit down near the bumper. The entire front of the vehicle, below, above and around the windscreen, was covered with huge lamps, and every single one was flashing, shooting dazzling beams into Billy and Hannah's eyes. Even from a distance, even in daylight, this felt to Hannah almost like staring into the sun. She couldn't see who was in the cab, but she could certainly hear, because from a pair of loudhailers on the roof, a voice so cold and steely you could have used it to slice a pumpkin boomed out.

'WHO IS THAT ... *PERSON* ... ON *MY* CAMEL?'

'Sorry,' said Billy, in Hannah's ear. 'You'd better go.'

'OK ... er ... how do I get down?'

'Like this.'

Billy lifted her off Narcissus's hump and dropped her onto the road. She landed like a sack of potatoes, that is if a sack of potatoes was capable of twisting its ankle but immediately standing up again and smiling bravely as if nothing was wrong.🐫

With the driver of the lorry watching, Billy seemed like a different person. All the sparkiness and humour on his face disappeared. As he nudged Narcissus back into motion with a click of his tongue, Hannah stared up at him, wondering why he was so scared of the man driving the lorry. It was as if just by looking at him, this person could make the real Billy disappear.

🐫This is a very special sack of potatoes we're talking about here, but let's not rule anything out. Life is full of surprises.

Just before he slipped away around the corner of the narrow road, heading towards town, Billy turned and gave her a quick secret wink.

'See you later,' he called. 'And don't forget what I told you.'

Hannah was not in the habit of forgetting anything (unless it was something boring, in which case she didn't so much forget it as just go deaf while it was being said) but she didn't understand what Billy's instructions meant.

While the caravan of caravans trundled past, before the lorry could get near, Hannah and Fizzer jumped over a hedge and skedaddled at top speed. (Well, Hannah's top speed. Fizzer was somewhere between a stroll and an amble.)

THREE

Whatever you do, don't enter the raffle

LATER THAT DAY, after the circus had rolled into the centre of Hannah's town and set up camp in the park, after the animals had been settled and fed, after a huge stew had been cooked on an open fire in an iron pot the size of a witches' cauldron and gobbled up in five minutes flat, the Shank troupe paraded along the high street to drum up some trade for the evening show.

At the front was Maurice, the trapeze artiste, whose name is pronounced Murrggghhhheeece, as if you are gargling an espresso of pond water. If you said his name without enough pond water in your gargle, Maurice pretended not to hear you. Maurice was French. In fact he was so proud of being French that he actually became slightly ratty if any other French people came within range, causing him to increase his Frenchness in order to ensure that he was always the most French person in his immediate vicinity. This was why he'd been forced to emigrate. Living with such a high level of competitive Frenchness in France itself was simply too exhausting.

Unconnected to this problematic patriotism, but at the very heart of his trapeze-artistry, was Maurice's curious habit of smearing himself in baby oil from head to toe before every performance or public appearance. He liked the way the theatre lights glistened against his muscled chest, which he shaved every morning with a (whisper it) ladies' razor. He just loved to be shiny.

The effect of his baby oil shine wasn't quite so impressive in daylight, but on the parade into town, Maurice more than made up for this by his unusual method of forward propulsion. He didn't walk; he didn't run; he didn't saunter, stride or march. He tumbled. Forward rolls and somersaults, back flips and midair twizzles, cartwheels and swallow dives

– these were Maurice's moves, and he choreographed them with casual perfection, his face puckered all the while into a wonky half-smile which seemed to say, 'Me? A genius of physical agility? The human form at its most exquisite? Masculinity raised to a superhuman level of perfection? Oh, no. You exaggerate. I'm just a humble Frenchman who happens to have been blessed with a few modestly dazzling skills.'

The only person in the circus who agreed with Maurice's opinion of his own genius was Irrrrrena, his Russian assistant who only ever wore the world's smallest bikini, except in mid-winter, when she added a dressing gown the size of a baby's cardigan.

Irrrrrena ran alongside Maurice, spreading her arms wide in *did-you-see-THAT!* amazement every time he did a move, following up with a circular clapping motion, as if she was stirring a huge saucepan containing a clap casserole. This was supposed to generate applause, and it usually worked. Irrrrrrrena was Maurice's trapeze assistant, choreographer, costumier, chef, bodyguard, driver, masseur, moustachier, talcum powderer, groomer-in-chief, personal trainer, psychotherapist, physiotherapist, aromatherapist and girlfriend. Like Maurice, Irrrrrrrena loved to glisten, except she had to settle for shine-free arms and legs, so she wouldn't be too slippery for him to throw her up in the air and catch her. Once, he squeezed her a little too tightly and she shot up in the air and got stuck in a tree. That lead to a huge row, because he wanted her to stop using baby oil altogether, but she thought it was unfair for him to be shinier than her.

Maurice was almost as competitive about shininess as he was about Frenchness. He was a very competitive man. On rare occasions that he met someone more competitive than himself, he even became competitive about being competitive.

Apart from the occasional dispute about the oiling issue, Maurice and Irrrrrena^{FR} seemed most of the time to be deeply in love. This made for quite a contrast with the twins, Hank and Frank, who

FR The number of 'R's is variable, depending on how well you know her, time of day and humidity.

were immediately behind them in the parade.

Hank and Frank had been working together since they were zero years old, and were often said to be the best twin-clown pairing since Huupi and Duupi, the Finn twins who had been tragically wiped out when a frying-pan-in-the-face gag was so perfectly executed that the laughter had triggered an avalanche, which sent them, and their whole Big Top, to the bottom of a half-frozen lake from which, it was said, bubbles of laughter still sometimes rose up to the surface, giggling as they burst into the air. But that's another story.

Hank and Frank simply didn't get on. They hadn't said a kind word to one another since . . . well . . . since they'd learned to talk. Things had started badly, when Hank was half-way born and Frank had pulled him back by the ankles because he wanted to come out first. Since then, year after year, they had only become more argumentative, but as their comedy routine revolved around throwing things at one another, whacking each other on the head and tripping one another over, the fact that their whole lives had been one long, ongoing bicker just added extra sparkle and conviction to their performance. Fighting, for Hank and Frank, was both a job and a hobby. And who can ask for more from life than that?

Behind the twins was Jesse, the Human Cannonball, in his trademark fur leotard. Following a crisis of conscience Jesse had recently switched to fake fur, but sadly he was allergic to polyester, and his new leotard made him one of the itchiest men in the world (which is an interesting claim to fame, but doesn't make for a circus act). No one knew how Jesse had become a Human Cannonball. He hated loud bangs, suffered from terrible vertigo, disliked travel, endured atrocious stage-fright and was generally afraid of almost everything including cats, spaghetti and train tickets. He was, frankly, in the wrong job.

There wasn't much for him to do on the parade except prance, show off his muscles, and scratch. Some places, no matter how itchy, just can't be scratched in public, so Jesse

was often cross-eyed with
the effort of keeping up a
standard of appropriate
public itching.

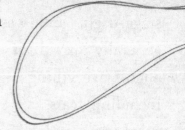

Behind Jesse strode
the entrepreneur, svengali,🎩 director, inspiration
and ringmaster of the circus, Billy's dad, Armitage
Shank. He wore a pair of red trousers that were so
tight you could read the date on the coins in his
pocket. His shirt was white and puffy, made of
fabric that billowed around him as if he was
walking around in a cloud of icing sugar. In his
right hand was a whip, which he cracked in the air
with flicks of his wrist so subtle the whip seemed
to be cracking itself.

And behind Armitage Shank, seemingly not
part of the parade at all, disguised in 'civilian'
clothes, was Billy. He was walking quietly along
with his hands in his pockets, scouring the ever-

🎩Hardly anyone actually knows what 'svengali' means, but that doesn't matter, because
just the sound of the word tells you everything you need to know. A svengali, as you can
probably guess, is somebody who is wise and important and powerful and ever so slightly
sinister.

growing crowd with an intense and studious gaze, as if he was searching for something, or someone. The strange thing was, he definitely appeared to be pretending he was nothing to do with the circus.

Hannah sprinted out of the house in her best (oldest) jeans and favourite (dirtiest) T-shirt, as soon as she heard the *ooohs* (of people watching Maurice's backflips), the *aaaahs* (as Jesse weightlifted a passer-by in each hand), the occasional *hmmmngg* (from people who were unaccountably distracted by Irrrrena) and a long, bubbling rise and fall of laughter (as Hank and Frank battered, bundled, beat, bruised, bonked, bashed and bamboozled one another with a variety of amusingly shaped implements).

The minute Hannah saw the parade, she understood. This was what Billy had been trying to explain. Shank's Impossible Circus didn't need to publicise their shows in advance, because they'd perfected a way of selling tickets on the day.

The leaping and weightlifting and whip-cracking and circular-clapping-in-a-tiny-bikini and bashy bamboozling soon drew a crowd that formed itself into a circle around a patch of previously unspectacular pavement space in the town square, which now realised with some excitement that it had become a stage.² Irrrrena did a few laps of the pavement-stage, pulling some people forward, nudging others back, until she had a neat circle. Then she clapped one last time, and all the performers slipped rapidly away, leaving a large crowd of people staring at a circle of empty pavement.

Just at the exact, precise and specific moment when anticipation started to dip, and people began to ask themselves why they were all staring interestedly at nothing whatsoever, like a regional

² It is hard to tell when a paving slab becomes excited, but if you look very, very carefully it is possible to spot the difference. There is a slight temperature rise and occasionally a jiggle. A clue is the sight of ants (who hate excitement) running for their lives, in search of somewhere boring.

conference of pavement-appreciators, Fingers O'Boyle leapt onto the stage.

Nobody knew where he had sprung from, since he hadn't been visible during the parade, and Fingers O'Boyle was clearly not the kind of person

who could blend into a crowd. Why? Because he
was dressed like a cross between a tramp and The
Emperor of the Empire of Lurid Show-offy Clothes.
Allow me to explain. I shall start at the bottom of
his outfit. Yellow patent leather (i.e. shiny shiny

shiny) shoes with stack heels made of transparent plastic, containing a ring of bright green frozen-in-time beetles. Knee socks, yellow with red polka dots. White plus fours (i.e. long shorts) so baggy and extravagant they should have been called plus sixty-eights. Above this, a flowing ankle-length coat which was halfway between a spectacular festive gown designed to honour the Goddess of Rainbows and a bunch of lurid rags held together with dodgy sewing, bits of glue and smears of dirt. The coat had actually started life in a production of *Joseph and his Technicolour Panopoly of Drippy Songs*, which was so bad Fingers had decided to spare the world any further performances by stealing the costumes. Since then, whenever Fingers found a scrap of interesting fabric, he'd snip a bit off and add it to the coat using whatever thread, glue or dirt came to hand.

Fingers' idea of 'finding' things was slightly

unusual. The concept of ownership was not one he strongly believed in. He once 'found' a piece of delightful purple paisley on the shirt of a woman standing in front of him in a bus queue. Being unusually dextrous, and handy with a pair of sharp scissors, Fingers had snipped out a square and skipped away before the woman had time to say 'What's that breeze on my back?' This is basically a long way of saying Fingers was a thief. Not your bog-standard grab-it-off-the-shelves-and-run-for-it thief, but a true magician in the art of making things disappear in front of your very eyes before you even notice they are gone.

It was this skill he used to hold the attention of the crowd assembled around him. His act, in short, went something like this: choose a volunteer from the crowd, chat to them, charm them, make them laugh, make everyone else laugh at them, do a couple of card tricks, then, just before you send them back to their place, casually say, 'Don't you want these?' before handing back watches, wallets, credit cards, wedding rings, and once (his *piece-de-resistance*) a pair of knickers to the embarrassed guest star.

WARNING TO READERS OF A SENSITIVE NATURE: WE ARE NOW ABOUT TO ATTEMPT A DANGEROUS ACTIVITY KNOWN AS A FLASHBACK. IF YOU ARE CHRONOLOGICALLY VULNERABLE, EASILY CONFUSED, OR ALLERGIC TO HICCUPS IN THE SPACE-TIME CONTINUUM, DO NOT ATTEMPT TO READ THE FOLLOWING PARAGRAPHS UNLESS YOU ARE WEARING THICK SUNGLASSES OR A SNORKEL (WITH MASK – FLIPPERS OPTIONAL).

Please cast your mind back roughly ten minutes or so in book-time. Are you there? Fingers O'Boyle is just stepping up onto the pavement-stage. A tiny line of ants is running away, screaming minuscule ant screams. Who do you think is his first 'member of the public' up on stage? Can you guess?

I don't know why I asked you that question, since I can't hear you. But if your answer was Billy, then you guessed correctly. If you guessed someone else, we can all just pretend that you like to shout out names randomly while you read books. It might be best to shout out another name now, to make this more convincing to passers-by.

Only one person notices that Billy isn't who he's pretending to be. Hannah. She has also noticed, with some surprise and horror, that while the other performers were gathering the crowd, Billy was working his way around the circle, slipping his delicate, fast-moving, not-very-clean hands into the pockets of the audience.

If Hannah hadn't become his friend earlier that day, she might have leapt out into the middle of the circle, stopped the show, and exposed Billy's thieving, but she sensed this wasn't what you should do to a friend, so she just watched anxiously as he pilfered items from the crowd.

She wasn't sure she was doing the right thing, since Billy had admitted the whole circus was on the run, and he certainly did not like the sound of the word 'police'. There was definitely something fishy going on.✒

While everyone else enjoyed the beginnings of the show, Hannah wrestled with her dilemma. Should she trust her instincts and trust Billy, or trust the fact that stealing was stealing was stealing? Because putting your hands into other people's pockets and walking away with their stuff – that's stealing.

Before she'd decided what to do, Billy was called up on stage as the first volunteer. During part of the act, at the exact moment when Fingers was pointing out that a missing ace of spades was stuck to a lamp post up above everyone's heads, Hannah

---

✒If this comment causes offence to any fish who happen to be reading this book, I apologise. My use of the term 'fishy' is not intended to be in any way disrespectful towards our ocean-dwelling friends.

saw, in the twinkle of an eye, a small, not-very-clean hand slip a large clutch of shiny objects into Fingers' pocket. These were the objects which in the course of the next half-hour were returned to their owners. While everyone else laughed and gasped with every new revelation, Hannah just sighed with relief.

FLASHBACK-PHOBICS AND SPACE-TIME STICKLERS CAN NOW REMOVE WHATEVER PROTECTIVE HEADGEAR THEY HAVE DONNED.

The show ended with more gymnastics and general circus hoopla, while Mr Shank sat behind a velvet-covered table, selling tickets for the evening's one-night-only performance. If he had been selling hot cakes to a town of cake-starved cake fanatics at the height of their annual Build A House Out Of Cakes Festival, he could hardly have sold tickets any faster.

Every ticket came with free entry to the Shank Entertainment Empire annual charity raffle, and Armitage was such a charming and debonair salesman that almost everyone happily put down their name and address, usually without even asking which charity was involved or what the prize might be.✷

Hannah did as she was told and didn't approach Billy, but as the crowd began to disperse, he suddenly appeared by her side.

'I saw you,' said Hannah.

'I know,' said Billy. 'I saw you seeing me. Thanks for not spoiling the show.'

'I was worried. I thought you were stealing. Especially after what you said.'

'What did I say?'

✷✷Let's have a little chat, down here at the bottom of the page where none of the characters can hear us. Would you like to know what the prize is? I'll give you a clue. It's not a prize at all. In fact, it is something rather horrible that nobody in their right mind would ever want, and even people in their wrong mind would try to avoid.

'You said you were on the run.'

'I told you that was a joke,' he said.

'But what if you telling me it was a joke was the joke?'

Billy narrowed his eyes and peered at Hannah as if he was examining her through a microscope. 'You're clever,' he said, 'but you think too much.'

'I don't think it's possible to think too much. Thinking's good.'

'Maybe you're right. Narcissus thinks all the time. But only about food.'

'Are you on the run or not? I want to know.'

'It's complicated. One day I'm going to get out, but I can't just yet.'

'What do you mean?' Hannah asked, feeling very confused.

'It's too difficult to explain. Do you want to come to the show tonight?'

'How much is it?'

'It's free.'

'So why are people queuing up to pay?'

'Because they're not you. Look in your pocket.'

Hannah slipped a hand into her jeans and pulled out a small square of card. A ticket! She unfolded it. Two tickets!

'It says it costs twenty pounds,' she said.

'I know. But to you, zero pounds. It's an apology.'

'For what?'

'For being shouted at earlier.'

'It wasn't you who shouted.'

'Well, you can give them back if you don't want them.'

'Of course I want them! Thanks very much. How did you get them in my pocket?'

Billy shrugged, grinned, and walked away. After a few steps, he turned back and casually said, 'I might be free later this afternoon, if you'd like to pop over.'

'OK,' she answered, and was about to ask him what time, but she sensed this wasn't how Billy thought. He didn't seem like a clock kind of a person. She'd just have to guess, and amble along when the time felt right.

'And whatever you do,' he whispered, 'don't enter the raffle.'

Then he was gone.

FOUR

Death by carrot

HANNAH TRIED TO PLAY IT COOL. She really did attempt to convince herself there was a way to fill the rest of the morning with something other than her new friend and his circus, but no dice. Since meeting Billy, even her most interesting possessions looked boring. She could find nothing to do. Nothing.☺ She shlumpfed round her room, feebly flopping on flat feet from one farcical fandango of fruitless futility to the next. A brother or sister might have helped to

---

☺Nothing nothing nothing. Not anything. Zero. Nil. Zilch. Naught. Nada. Niente. Diddly-squat. Nothing.

distract her, but Hannah was an only child, so the only person keeping her company was a voice in her head which spent the whole morning shouting, 'VISIT BILLY! VISIT BILLY! VISIT HIM NOW!'

Hannah got so bored she spent more than twenty minutes watching TV, which was a strange thing to do, since the TV was off. This was a house rule. No TV before that mysterious tipping point at the end of the afternoon when parents basically give up.

'Are you watching TV?' Hannah's mum yelled from the kitchen.

'Sort of,' said Hannah.

'What do you mean, "sort of"? Either you are or you aren't.'

'Well, I sort of am and sort of aren't.'

'Are you being cheeky?' shouted Hannah's dad from the cupboard under the stairs.

An obvious reply popped into Hannah's head:

'Sort of.' She knew she'd be in trouble if she said this, but she could feel the words bouncing around her mouth like two kittens fighting in a paper bag.

Hannah's Dad spent a lot of time in the cupboard under the stairs. Nobody knew why. It was where he mended things and broke things, and tried to mend the things he had broken, but more often ending up breaking the things he had mended.

This is what he did at the weekend, anyway. From Monday to Friday he worked as an accountant, which basically means that he did maths all day, every day. Just the thought of this gave Hannah the wollycobbles.✷ Hannah's mum, by the way, was a Health and Safety Consultant, which means that she spent all day, every day, teaching people how to be more cautious, unadventurous and fearful. I won't go on about this topic, since I don't want to be a gloombucket, but suffice to say, Hannah was something of a

---

✷ Wollycobbles are similar to collywobbles but MUCH WORSE.

disappointment to her parents.

Hannah decided that the only way to avoid getting told off again was to run back up to her room. She looked in the mirror and began to practise Billy's mysterious-visitor/jellyfish-attack face, inventing a couple of significant improvements, which she decided she could show him later if the conversation flagged.

She pulled down the skin under her right eye and examined the crescent of pink flesh this exposed. *I diagnose*, she thought to herself, in a doctory voice, *an advanced case of SHD: Summer Holiday Disorder.*

SYMPTOMS: *Listlessness; boredom; more boredom; lack of ideas; inertia; apathy; feebleness of the imagination; dislike of all human beings; disinterest in all objects; hatred of the outdoors, the indoors, and doors in general; sleepiness; insomnia; boredom, boredom* *and more boredom.*

CURE: *There is no cure. Apart from teleporting yourself out of your boring life into the life of someone more interesting than yourself.*

PROBLEM WITH THIS CURE: *There's no such thing as teleporting.*

At this moment, thinking about teleporting, thinking about other lives lived by other people, something went *pfffzinggg!* in Hannah's brain. Her eyes darted towards the clock beside her bed, on which she was ecstatic to see the numbers 1,1,5 and 3. Yes, it was 11:53. She stared, transfixed, and waited.

Several aeons later, the time was 12:01. That, technically, was the afternoon. She could visit Billy now, without appearing desperate or overkeen. In fact, she'd be at least one minute late, which would seem kind of cool and easy-going.

On second thoughts, or six hundred and ninety-eighth thoughts, depending on whether you start counting at 12:01 or at the beginning of her SHD flopfest, Hannah decided that perhaps the best thing would be to take a roundabout route to a hidden spot at the edge of the park, and just see what the circus people were up to. Then she'd be able to pick her moment and casually turn up when Billy wasn't too busy for her. If she was there, rather than in her room, at least she wouldn't be bored. And if Billy really was too busy, she could always talk to Narcissus. With this in mind, she loaded up her pockets with carrots (which looked like the best option from the fridge for a camel; better, at least, than Cheddar, taramasalata or leftover baked beans) and set off.

It was a hot day. But that's enough about the weather.

Moments after leaving the house, she heard the

faint *click-clack* of dog claws against pavement. There, at her side, was Fizzer. His tail was up, in that perky but aloof fashion unique to him, which seemed to mean, 'What kept you? It's 12:03 already.'

'Where did you spring from?' said Hannah.

Fizzer didn't answer, partly because he liked to retain his air of mystery, and partly because he was a dog, and therefore couldn't talk. ⋙

'Let's go,' she said. 'What do you think Billy's up to?'

Again, Fizzer kept his opinions to himself.

Once she had reached the park, Hannah, who was a highly skilled tree climber, took up a perch in her favourite twisty oak, from which she had a perfect vantage point looking over the preparations for the night's performance.

Fizzer, who did not count tree climbing among his list of talents, stayed at the bottom of the trunk,

---

⋙ 'Speaking of which,' I hear you say, 'You've still not told us who Fizzer is. Where does he keep appearing from? Where does he go?' Patience, my friends. Patience.

which he proceeded to sniff with great interest.

The Big Top was already up, and it was, as you might expect, big. It was made of red and white stripy fabric which made the whole thing look like the world's largest sweet. All the performers were streaming in and out of the enormous lorry, carrying props and costumes and lights and microphones and cables and large wooden crates. Everyone moved fast and smoothly, seeming to know exactly what should go where without any discussion. The whole operation was impressively efficient, which wasn't a word Hannah had previously associated with circuses.

She stared at this ballet of heavy lifting, riveted. Not literally. I'm not suggesting that a ship-builder arrived and riveted her to the tree. It is illegal to rivet people to trees, and for good reason. The point is that Hannah found this process, the setting-up of the circus, enthralling. In

fact, although other
people might have
seen it as just a line
of weirdly dressed
people unloading a
lorry, Hannah thought
it was one of the most
beautiful and fascinating
endeavours she had ever witnessed.

There was something about that combination of anarchy and organisation, of freedom and togetherness, that looked to her like a vision of the perfect way to live.

Her life at the moment contained no anarchy, not much organisation, hardly any freedom and precious little togetherness. If she could have teleported herself into somebody else's life, she knew who she'd choose. Billy. Without a moment's hesitation, without a shadow of a doubt, without a flicker of indecision. Billy's life was the life she wanted.

Hannah was not the complaining sort, but if you had offered her ten words to describe the town where she lived, she would have chosen dull, dull, dull, dull, dull, dull, dull, dull, dull and dull. She didn't know how she knew it, or why she thought it, or what it really meant, but for as long as she could remember Hannah had felt, in the core of her being, that she'd been born into the wrong family in the wrong place in the wrong house with the wrong friends and the wrong clothes and the wrong bedroom and, oh, you get the point. Things just felt *wrong*. Hannah loved life, but she'd always been haunted by a curious sense that the life she had was not the life she was meant to have.

Fizzer looked up at Hannah with a worried expression on his face, not because he thought she might fall out of the tree, but because he knew this was a momentous moment. He knew he was lookng up at a girl who was losing her heart. Not in a soppy way, not in a romantic way, not even to a person, but to an idea.

Life is long and contains many twists and turns. Fizzer could see that Hannah, up in that tree, was in the middle of a particularly twisty turn. At this instant, she was seeing, for the first time, where life was going to take her. (Or, if you prefer, where she was going to take her life.)

How did Fizzer know this?

Because he did. Because he was that kind of dog, and he understood Hannah better than her parents (which wasn't very hard), better than her friends (which wasn't particularly hard, either), better even, perhaps, than Hannah understood herself (which was a significant achievement for a canine, but Fizzer, as you know, was special). He also sensed that this twisty turn was something Hannah needed to discover by herself, so he wandered off to investigate a nearby bush.

When the lorry was fully unloaded, the unloaders disappeared into the tent, and Hannah turned her attention to Billy. He wasn't part of the lifting and carrying operation. He was circling around the Big Top, hammering in metal pegs with a huge mallet and attaching guy ropes, which he then tightened with something that looked like a crowbar. Hannah found herself wondering if he might like some help, and also if there was such a thing as a Small Top.

She swung herself down from the oak and sauntered over. Sauntering was something she had been practising lately, and she felt she'd got rather good at it, but Billy didn't seem to notice.

'Oh, hi,' he said, sounding pleased to see her (but not too pleased, or not pleased enough).

'You want a hand?' she said.

'Are you any good with a sledgehammer?'

'Not sure. Doesn't look too hard.'

'Have a go.'

Hannah grabbed the hammer, gripping it tightly as she realised that it would take all her strength to lift it off the ground. Summoning every ounce of muscle-power, she swung her arms and raised the hammer high above her head. It had looked easy when she watched Billy. But there was obviously a knack, an element of momentum that was crucial to the whole procedure, because no sooner did the hammer go up, than it seemed to decide on its own to go down again, without any negotiation as to

where it was going to land. The hammer crashed to the ground, behind Hannah, dragging her down with it, flat on her back.

'You OK?' asked Billy.

'*Hhhh gggg khkhkhkh*,' Hannah replied. It wasn't easy to get words out when you'd just lost a wrestling match with a chunk of metal on a stick.

'It's harder than it looks. How about I do the hammering and you do the guy ropes?'

'Good plan,' said Hannah, standing and dusting herself down.

Billy swung and whacked, with easy skill, and Hannah followed him round the tent, tightening and tugging. They moved much faster than Billy had managed on his own, and he thanked her for her help with a pat on the arm that almost knocked her over again. He was small, but stronger than he looked.

'I brought something for Narcissus,' said

Hannah, pulling a pair of carrots from her pocket.

'That's very nice of you,' said Billy, 'except for one thing.'

'What?'

'He hates carrots. Detests them. Loathes them. If you so much as show him a carrot, he goes mental.'

'Really? What does he eat, then?'

'Pellets.'

'Pellets of what?'

'Don't know. Stuff. They look almost the same as his poo, which is weird.'

'Don't you ever give him a treat?'

'Oh, yeah. It sounds strange, but his favourite treats are Cheddar, baked beans and taramasalata.'

'You're kidding! But that's . . . !'

'That's what?'

'Never mind. Hard to explain.'

'I love them, though,' said Billy.

'What?'

'Carrots.' With that, he took both vegetables from Hannah and bit the tops off with one double-carrot-biting munch.

'I haven't peeled them,' she said. 'Or washed them.'

'Oh, a bit of mud never killed anyone. Adds to the flavour if you ask me.'

Billy swallowed, and was about to take another double-carrot bite, when his face suddenly froze. He doubled over, grabbing his stomach, then lurched upright again. His face was red, his eyes squeezed tight shut, his mouth open in a silent howl of horror. He froze for a moment, then his whole body began to spasm, twitch, leap, flop, flip and flap, while his throat emitted a series of splutters, gurgles and chokes. It didn't take Hannah long to realise that Billy was dying.

Not really dying.

Pretending to die. It was an impressive performance, which came to a climax with Billy flat on his back on the grass, while each limb one by one shuffled off this mortal coil.⁹

'Not bad,' said Hannah.

Billy didn't answer, which perhaps wasn't very surprising given that he was dead.

Hannah walked over and gave him a poke. He didn't respond, so she lifted his carrot-holding arm, which remained limp, and took a bite from the carrots that he was still gripping.

'Nice,' she said, chomping noisily. 'Delicious.' *Munch munch munch.* 'Crunchy.' *Crunch crunch crunch.* 'Chewy.' *Chew chew chew.* 'But a bit . . . a bit . . .' *choke, cough, splutter,* 'a bit . . . a bit . . .' *gasp, spit, wheeze,* 'a bit . . . ' *pant, heave, convulse,* 'a bit . . . MUUDDDYYYYYYYYYYYYYY!'

Hannah gave a full minute to her 'I can't breathe' routine, before launching into a beached fish

---

⑨'What is a mortal coil,' you ask, 'and why is he shuffling off it?' This is a posh way of saying that Billy's snuffed it, or pretended to, and has done so in such a theatrical way that he deserves a theatrical description of his efforts. I've nicked this phrase from a play called *Hamlet*, so if you think it's no good don't blame me.

number which involved lying flat on the ground, flailing every part of the body that can be flailed and a few that usually can't. After this, she went into a kind of electric shock full-body breakdown that involved grunting, mouth-frothing, tongue-waggling, eye-rolling and a fair amount of human pogo-sticking. When she felt she'd hit a dramatic peak she stopped, went rigid, and toppled to the ground like a felled tree.

Billy, fully recovered from his fatal carrot incident, gave a round of applause. Hannah stood and bowed, first to Billy, then to an imaginary audience all around her, not forgetting to wave modestly to the people up high in the cheap seats.

'You want to take Narcissus some pellets?' said Billy.

FIVE

The tragic tale of Esmeralda Espadrille

SNUGGLED IN THE CORNER of Narcissus's cage (which was so cosy it felt more like a hotel room), Hannah asked the questions that had been troubling her for most of the day. 'Was that Armitage Shank who shouted at us this morning?'

Billy nodded.

'You looked really scared. Is he mean to you?'

Billy shrugged.

'When you said that one day you're going to get out, were you talking about running away?'

Billy's chin moved ever so slightly upwards and to the left, which appeared to be both a nod and a shrug.

'You're supposed to run away *to* the circus, not from it.'

'I *would* run away to the circus. I could never become a civilian. Yuk! No offence. What I want is to run away from this circus to another one. My dad's one.'

'But you're Billy Shank. Heir to the Shank Entertainment Empire. I thought Mr Shank was your dad.'

'Not my real dad. He's just my circus dad.'

'What does that mean?'

'It means Armitage booted out my real dad and twisted his circus into what it is now.'

'Which is what?'

'I can't really say.'

'Why not?'

'I can't say.'

'Is it something to do with why you're on the run?'

Billy nodded.

'Are you always on the run?'

Billy nodded.

For a short while,⊕ they sat in silence. Then Billy said, 'Do you want me to tell you the whole story? About my dad and everything.'

'Oh, yes. If you don't mind.'

'Usually I do. It's not something I like talking about, and I'm not really allowed to tell anyone, either. You're different, though.'

'Thanks. Different from what?'

'Other civilians. But you have to promise not to cry.'

'Is it a very sad story?'

'Tragic.'

Not crying was something Hannah was not good at. In fact, just the thought of listening to a

---

⊕A short while is precisely seven seconds. A while is sixteen seconds. A long while is one and a half minutes. This has been agreed at an international conference of timekeepers. Ages is thirty-seven minutes, blooming ages is fifty-two minutes and yonks is 2.3 years. Decision on a final definition of jiffy has been delayed until next year, due to an unseemly episode involving heckling, a jug of iced water and a frenzied kerfuffle of fisticuffs.

sad story made her want to cry. The thought of a tragic story – a tragic story that had actually happened to Billy and his family – well, that had an instant effect.

Hannah began to cry. Not sobby, snotty, snorty crying, just a silent little leak from the corner of her left eye, which was always the weepier of the two. Her right eye was as hard as nails.

'Are you crying already?' said Billy.

'No,' sniffed Hannah.

'I haven't even started yet!'

'It's just hay fever.'

'No, it isn't.'

'Maybe I'm allergic to camels.'

'I don't think you are. I think you're allergic to sad stories.'

'I'm not wet. I just cry easily. I don't know why. The thought of other people being unhappy, especially people I like, always sets me off. It's dodgy eye plumbing, that's all.'

'OK,' said Billy. 'Cry if you really have to. But try and wait till I get to the sad bit.'

'I'll do my best.'

Billy took a deep breath and began to speak in a slow, sombre tone. 'This whole circus used to belong to my family. My *real* family. Back then, it was Espadrille's Impossible Circus. My mum was Esmeralda Espadrille.'

He paused expectantly. A hush filled the cage – a strange kind of hush, of a variety you may not have heard – that of nobody talking, accompanied by distant birdsong and not-at-all-distant camel snoring. A camel snore, by the way, sounds like a man sawing through a tree trunk. In other words, this was a rather noisy variety of hush,[zz] and the longer it went on, the more confused Hannah became.

'Why have you stopped?' she said, eventually.

[zz] The snore of a female camel, curiously enough, sounds exactly like a woman sawing through a tree trunk. This has been conclusively proved by the experiments of Professor Zzzz at the Western Sahara College of Lumberjacking, though a rival study by Doctor Hump of the Saskatchewan Institute of Dromedary Studies disputes these findings. Hump and Zzzzz regularly exchange angry letters.

'Esmeralda Espadrille!' Billy repeated. 'The trapeze artist!'

'Er . . .'

'*Esmeralda Espadrille! The only person ever to do a back somersault from trapeze to trapeze with a double pike, triple flip-flop and* quadruple wing-ding! Queen of the air! Bird-woman supreme!'

'Oh!' said Hannah, with a polite attempt to sound like she knew what he was talking about. 'Esmeralda Epsadrille! The trapeze artist! She was your mum?'

'Yes! And you know what happened to her, don't you?'

'Er...'

'The papers never told the full story. You see, this was my mum and dad's circus for years, and before that my grandparents', but Mum and Dad weren't very good with the money side. They just spent everything they made on the show, and on looking after the animals, so they got into debt. They tried to borrow to keep things afloat, but going to a bank to borrow money for a circus is like going into a tiger cage and asking for a massage. It's not going to happen. In the end, there was only one person who'd lend them money. Armitage.'

'Armitage?'

'Armitage Shank.'

'Your circus dad.'

'Exactly.'

'I still don't know what that means.'

'I'm coming to that. First you need to know who he is.'

'A crook?'

'Exactly. You're quick.' Billy smiled in approval. 'Armitage Shank has been on the circuit for years, running dodgy circuses which open up and shut down, then open up again somewhere else under a new name. He's always on the run, and the police are always after him because of his shady deals and dodgy practices and general crookery. Basically the first and only rule of the circus world is Stay Away From Armitage Shank.'

'So why did your parents ask him for money?'

'It was the only way to keep the circus going. It was either take Armitage's money, or sell everything, give up and move into a . . . a . . . I can't say it.'

'A house?'

'That's the word. I mean, it was the worst thing that could possibly happen. It was the nightmare that makes you tremble and sweat and scream, but on the brink of becoming reality. We would have had to become civilians. *Bleuuuurrrrgggghhhh!* No offence!'

'So you had to take his money?'

'Exactly. That was when we became Shank's Impossible Circus, and my parents became his employees. It was Armitage who made Mum get rid of the safety net. He said it spoiled the excitement. And I suppose you know the rest.'

Hannah didn't know the rest, but with an awful sensation in her stomach she felt she might be able to guess. Billy wasn't crying, though, and Esmeralda was his mum, so Hannah knew she mustn't, either. Using all her mental strength, she clamped down on her tear ducts.

'My dad was the catcher,' Billy continued. 'It wasn't his fault. I mean, you can't get everything perfect every single night – that's why you need a net – but he never got over the guilt. His main thing in the show was juggling, and after the funeral he just couldn't do it any more. He had the jitters. He kept dropping things. Eventually Armitage sacked him and Dad had to leave. I wanted to go with him, but Dad wouldn't let me. He said he didn't have anywhere to live, or any way to make a living, and he wouldn't know how to look after me. He told me to stay with the circus, and he promised that as soon as he could, he'd come and get me. He promised that he'd get back on his feet, but he needed to know I was safe, and looked after, and this circus was the only place he knew where that would happen. Then he went, and my name was changed to Billy Shank, because Armitage doesn't have any real children and he thought having a son in the show would be good for his image.'

'He changed your name? He can't do that!'

'It's only a stage name. The one I had before was, too, so it doesn't make much difference. You don't think my mum was born Esmeralda Espadrille, do you?'

'I suppose not.'

'Her real name was something like Wendy Dunn. I'm not even sure. My dad was Ernesto Espadrille, but off stage everyone called him Clive.'

'That's the saddest thing I've ever heard,' said Hannah.

'It's just a name.'

'Not the name. The rest of it.'

'Oh. I suppose it is pretty bad. Thanks for not crying.'

Hannah shrugged. She didn't know what to say. Billy wasn't looking at her any more. He was scrunching up bits of hay and tossing them at his feet.

'The past is the past,' said Billy, after a while. 'And I know Dad will come and get me eventually. What upsets me now is the stealing.'

'The stealing?'

'WHAT DID YOU SAY?'

Billy and Hannah both jumped. Neither of them had heard him coming. Neither of them had seen the door open. They just heard the voice; that icy, terrifying voice, right there in the cage with them, bawling those four words with eye-popping fury. Hannah turned and found herself staring up at Armitage Shank. His moustache was still waxed, but other than that he was now in his off-stage outfit: a pink velour tracksuit and lime-green flip-flops. It isn't easy to look scary in a pink velour tracksuit and lime-green flip-flops, but Armitage managed it.

Hannah looked back at Billy, whose mouth was opening and closing with no sound coming out.

'WELL?' Armitage demanded.

'Healing,' said Billy, quickly. 'I said Narcissus's paw is *healing*.'

'Hmmmm,' said Armitage, turning his attention

to Hannah, eyeing her up and down as if she was a corn on the cob and he was pondering which end to gobble first. 'Who's this?' he sneered. 'A new *friend*?'

You may have noticed that dog walkers usually carry small plastic bags. You may also have noticed the rather unusual way that dog walkers carry

these bags when they are full, using only the tips of their fingers, as if they don't really want to be holding them. This is the way Armitage pronounced the word *friend*.

Billy didn't reply. He shuffled further back into the corner of the cage. Hannah felt herself doing the same thing.

Armitage looked at Hannah and spoke again, quietly now, but his quiet voice was somehow even scarier than his loud one. 'Because you ought to know that we don't have *friends* here. You people aren't our *friends.* You're our audience.'

Hannah cleared her throat. Her voice felt wobbly and thin, but she tried to speak as confidently as she could. 'Mr Shank,' she said, 'I don't mean to be rude, but I'm afraid you're mistaken, because Billy is my friend and I'm his.'

Armitage blinked at Hannah, appearing surprised that a creature so insignificant was even capable of speech, let alone of contradicting him.

'I beg your pardon?' he asked, in a tone of voice that used politeness in the way chefs use a cleaver.

'Pfffffffffp,' said Narcissus. And not with his mouth.

An extraordinary smell filled the cage, a cross between tear gas, sewage, curdled milk, egg sandwich and pickled herring. Hannah's eyes began to run, her nose streamed and her throat constricted. Armitage coughed, his stomach jerking as if he was struggling not to vomit. Billy didn't move, apart from a faint twitch of one nostril. Over the years, he had developed an immunity – almost a fondness – for Narcissus's gastric releases.

'And we've got some important things to do,' Hannah continued, encouraged by the camel's contribution to her argument. 'So if you'll excuse us, I'm afraid we have to go.'

Hannah reached out and grabbed Billy's hand. It felt cold and stiff, but she gripped hard and pulled, yanking him onto his feet and hauling him out of the cage.

Armitage spun on his heel and sprinted after them, but within seconds a dog leapt out from under a caravan and grabbed him by the leg of his tracksuit, toppling him into a patch of mud.🐕

'My tracksuit!' he yelped. 'MY TRACKSUIT! MY TRACKSUIT!'

If there was one thing Armitage hated even

🐕 You know which dog, don't you? Of course you do.

more than being contradicted by children, gassed by camels and outwitted by civilians, it was getting his clothes dirty.

Hannah and Billy darted across the park, running as fast as they could, out of sight and into the trees. They didn't stop until they reached Hannah's secret hideaway high up in the oak.

From far away, they could hear the distant sound of a tiny voice shouting very loudly.

'MY TRACKSUUUUUUUUUUUUUUUUUUUIIIIIIIIIIIIIIIIT!!!'

'I can't believe you did that,' said Billy, when he eventually got his breath back.

'Neither can I,' said Hannah.

'I've never seen anyone stand up to him before.'

'Really?'

'Never,' he said solemnly.

'What do you think he'll do?'

'What can he do? He doesn't even know who you are.'

Hannah looked down, her eye drawn by the casual, loping arrival of Fizzer, who had a scrap of pink velour dangling from his mouth.

'How much of a crook is he?' asked Hannah. 'What's really going on? Why is everyone so scared of him?'

And that's when Billy told her what was going to happen later in the evening, during the show, revealing to her every element of the dastardly, devious, deceitful, dishonest, devilish plan Armitage Shank had put into place. Billy had never before told anyone about the circus's criminal activities, because he knew it was the very secretest secret. If he was caught talking to any civilian about it, he'd be thrown out on the streets. But he trusted Hannah. There was something special about her. And he had a strange feeling – just a hint of a whisper of an inkling – that she was the kind of person who might be willing to help him.

Listening to the details of Armitage Shank's scheme, Hannah could hardly believe her ears. She was amazed. She was horrified. She was gobsmacked and flabbergasted and gobgasted and flabbersmacked.

Billy knew she'd be shocked, but the thing he didn't guess was what she would say in response. The words that came out of her mouth were, in fact, the last thing he expected.

'We have to stop it,' she said, without even a moment's thought.

Hannah had an unusually strong sense of what was right and what was wrong, and when one of them pretended to be the other, she never just stood back and watched.

'We can't,' replied Billy. 'It's not possible.'

'Everything's possible. You should know that more than anyone.'

'Why?'

'Think who you work for.'

'That's just a name.'

'Then think what you do. You live in a different place every night and you make a living by amazing people and you ride a camel and you dress yourself in curtains and your mum knew how to do a back somersault with a double pike and triple flip-flop and quadruple wing-ding!'

'Yes, but . . .'

'But what?'

'If you get on the wrong side of Armitage, you're done for. He's dangerous.'

'We can be dangerous, too, if we put our minds to it.'

'How?'

'I think I've got a plan,' she said, a mischievous glint sparkling in her eyes. 'Do you know how to drive a lorry?'

'A lorry?'

'*The* lorry. The enormous lorry. Can you drive it?'

SIX

Two plans take shape

HANNAH FACED A CONUNDRUM in four parts.

1. SHE NEEDED TO GO TO THE CIRCUS.

2. SHE WOULDN'T BE ALLOWED TO GO ON HER OWN, SO SHE NEEDED AN ADULT.

3. IN ORDER TO COMPLETE HER PLAN, SHE NEEDED AN ADULT WHO WOULDN'T NOTICE IF SHE SLIPPED AWAY DURING THE SHOW.

4. UNFORTUNATELY, NOBODY IN HER IMMEDIATE FAMILY WAS BLIND.

Tricky. But as you will remember, for Hannah nothing was impossible. And in this case, she quickly realised that her problem had one very simple solution: Granny.

Granny loved outings, particularly outings that gave you an excuse to buy sweets, so the circus was perfect. More important than the fact that Granny liked circuses (and that Hannah liked Granny) was a particular habit of Granny's, which on this occasion would come in extremely useful. If you took Granny anywhere and the lights dimmed, Granny fell asleep. Even if you took her nowhere and just dimmed the lights in the sitting room, Granny still fell asleep.

In bed, the lights trick didn't work. Granny, oddly enough, was a terrible insomniac. But put her in a chair, more or less anywhere, and if it got even slightly dark, Granny was guaranteed to doze off.

It was only a short walk to Granny's house, and when Hannah got there, she could hear the TV blaring through the front windows. Hannah pressed the bell hard, partly because Granny's hearing wasn't the best, partly because she knew she might well be asleep. After several long presses, and a few knocks on the window, Granny eventually came to the door.

'Oh, Hannah, love! It's you!'

'It is,' said Hannah, giving her a hug.

'I dozed off!' said Granny, who was surprised every time it happened. Granny often seemed to think she was twenty-five, as if the last fifty years hadn't really happened. 'Come in come in come in,' said Granny. 'I've got a bag of mint imperials that's just begging to be finished.'

Hannah came in and politely accepted a mint imperial, even though she thought they tasted like lumps of baked toothpaste.

'I can't stay long,' said Hannah, 'but I've got a present for you. A ticket to the circus. We can go together.'

'Oooh!' said Granny. 'How wonderful! Candy floss!'

'I have to dash. I'll come back and get you after tea.'

'Lovely.'

Then Hannah ran home, to make preparations for the evening's escapade.

✳

Meanwhile, the circus troupe had gathered round in the Big Top to talk through Armitage's arrangements. The running order for the show was usually the same, but for every performance the plan was different.

Why?

Because putting on the show was only half the job.

Or rather, the show the audience saw was only half the operation. It was what they didn't see that made Armitage Shank his money. And the only thing Armitage loved more than showing off was money. Money money money, sweeter than honey, cuter than a bunny, funnier than funny. He just looooooooooooooved money. He'd been like that since he was a child. When he was only six, his pet dog had a litter of puppies, which Armitage had named Cash, Wonga, Dough, Loot, Dosh, Moolah, Spondoolicks and Interest. After a couple of weeks, he sold them.

That afternoon, Armitage had done what he always did when the circus arrived in a new place. After the parade, after selling tickets and signing people up for the raffle, Armitage took a little tour of the town with a map in one hand and the list of raffle addresses in the other. Where the address looked like a large, or well furnished, or generally prosperous-seeming house, Armitage marked his map with a red cross.✗

As Armitage went through the running order

✗ Psst! Have you guessed what the prize-that-isn't-a-prize is yet? If you have, you are very clever. If you haven't, you are possibly also clever, but are lacking insight into the criminal mind, and into the techniques of burglary. Ooops! I've given it away. If you still haven't guessed now, you should probably rule out a career in the police force.

with his cast, everyone looked carefully at the map he handed out, which had a blue circle for the Big Top in the middle, and in the nearby streets a cluster of red crosses. Each performer was assigned

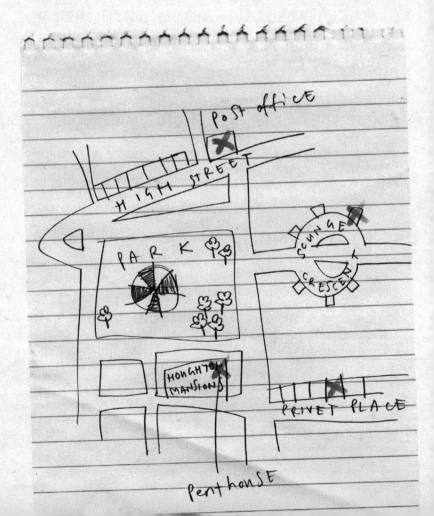

a house, and a gap of thirty minutes off-stage time when it was their job to nip out, find the house (which of course would be empty, because the occupants were at the circus), and rob it.

Hank and Frank were assigned 23 Privet Place; Maurice and Irrrrena were given the cat-burglary job on the penthouse apartment in Houghton Mansions; Jesse was in charge of the bungalow on Scunge Crescent; and the top team, Armitage and Fingers O'Boyle, would be working together to do over the Post Office, using the troupe's signature trick – a routine so outrageously, audaciously, courageously mendacious that you could almost, but not quite, describe it as impossible.

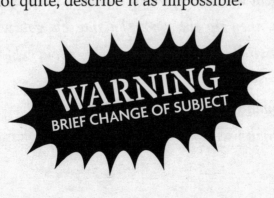

WARNING
BRIEF CHANGE OF SUBJECT

Every year, every car in the country goes to a garage to be serviced. A mechanic lifts the bonnet, rummages around in the engine, checks everything is OK, then gives you a certificate to carry on driving for another year without worrying about what is making the car go. I am now going to lift the bonnet of this book for a moment, and point something out that you may or may not have noticed, depending on whether you are a bonnet-lifting kind of person. Whoever you are, you cannot fail to have realised that Hannah and Armitage were, essentially, opposites.

Hannah, you will recall, took questions of right and wrong very seriously. Armitage, by contrast, liked to shove right and wrong into a liquidiser, make soup out of them, then tip the whole lot into his gob without giving two hoots, or even one hoot, about which was which.

Hannah was kind; Armitage was mean.

Hannah was modest; Armitage was arrogant.

Hannah was generous; Armitage was greedy.

Hannah liked apples; Armitage liked pears.

But when it came to this one word – impossible – they were the same. For both of them 'impossible' was just a challenge. They couldn't hear those four syllables without trying to figure out a plan for how to get rid of the 'im'.

This connection may just be a coincidence. On the other hand, it may not be. But going back to that first hand again, it might be. Or not.

That's all. Bonnet down. Off you go.

SEVEN

Are you . . . by any chance . . . ready?

HANNAH ARRIVED AT THE CIRCUS early, partly to have time to scope out the Big Top, partly to give herself a chance to get through the mound of candy floss she knew Granny would buy her. It's important to have at least half an hour between getting a candy floss from Granny and trying to watch a show, because when you are given something to hold that is roughly the size of a family car, you need to eat a large chunk before you will be able to see past it. There was a rumour that Granny once nearly suffocated herself at the cinema, when she dozed off during a matinee showing of *Charlie and the Chocolate Factory*, underneath an XXX-large bucket of sweet popcorn. When those things tip, it's pretty much like an avalanche. And as everyone knows, you can't outrun an avalanche, especially when you're asleep.

'Well, isn't this a treat?' said Granny, going at her candy floss with the speed and power of a garden strimmer.

'Mmm,' said Hannah, craning her neck to look around the Big Top, searching for the best exit route, hoping all the while that she might catch a glimpse of Billy.

Billy, meanwhile, was having a crisis of conscience. He knew that going along with Hannah's plan was the right thing to do, but he'd spent most of his life being taught that the wrong thing was the right thing, and vice versa, which left him scared, skewered, skittled, scuttled and skedaddled by the idea of standing up to Armitage Shank.

Even now, minutes before the curtain was due to go up on the show, Billy wasn't sure he could really go through with it.

He needed to talk to someone. So he went to visit Narcissus. Camels, in Billy's experience, were always good listeners. Narcissus would understand, and perhaps even dispense some advice.

Narcissus's advice, in the end, was a burp so stinky you could have used it to melt a post box. Then Billy heard the music start, and he knew the show was about to begin. Very soon he had to decide one way or the other. Was he in or was he out?

By the time the lights went down, Granny had already finished her candy floss and was enthusiastically licking the stick, fearless of splinters. After seventy-odd years of scorching hot tea, there wasn't much a mere splinter could do to hurt her well-seasoned tongue. And the candy-flossy stick just tasted sooooooo good, almost better than the floss itself, the woody notes and rough texture adding an ineffable✿ earthiness to that delicious sweetness.

Hannah had finished roughly a quarter of hers, but with darkness now filling the auditorium, she decided she could drop it under her seat without hurting Granny's feelings or seeming ungrateful.

After a rumble and blare of drum rolls and trumpets, a circle of light popped up in the middle of the ring. Hannah leaned forward in her seat. She didn't know why, but there was something exciting about a dark space, filled with silent people, staring at an empty circle of light. Everyone was looking at the same thing, and even though

---

✿Ineffable means indescribable. But once you have used this word, you have described the thing you are saying you can't describe, so it is therefore a pointless term and should probably be removed from all dictionaries. There is really no excuse for using it in a book, in particular a book for children. My reason for using it here is, frankly, ineffable.

the thing they were looking at was nothing more than a disc of sawdust, the wait for something to happen filled the tent with an electricity of anticipation.

The music stopped. Hannah waited for someone to appear in the light. Everyone waited. Everyone waited just that little bit longer than they all thought they'd have to wait, leaning further and further forward in their seats, until the light suddenly flicked off, for one-and-a-half blinks, before flicking on again to reveal Armitage Shank. He was wearing his billowy white shirt and tighter-than-tight trousers, sporting shoes that were pointy enough to dip in ink and use as a pen. He stood motionless, his body facing forwards, his head sideways. Both arms were above his head, clutching a whip.

Slowly, Armitage straightened his neck to face the audience.

◀▭ 'Sporting', in this context, is a verb. I should make it clear that the shoes Armitage is sporting are not sporting shoes, and never could be, unless the sport was competitive foot-only balloon bursting, or a how-far-can-you-point-without-using-your-hands contest. Just to make sure there's no confusion, the point is that he's not sporting sporting shoes, he's sporting non-sporting shoes.

'Are you ready?' he said, in a voice so quiet that everybody heard, but thought they might not have. Bit by bit, the circle of light around him began to swell.

'Are you ready?' he repeated, a shade louder.

As the circle of light got bigger, Armitage began to pace around the edge of the illuminated space, staring at the audience. While he walked, it somehow seemed as if he caught the eye of every single member of the audience, one by one, giving them an individual stare, as he asked them, once again, if they were ready.

'Well, *are* you?' he said, leaping into the air and landing with his legs apart, cracking his whip once, twice, three times to the left, the right, and up into the air.

'Yes,' said a couple of weak voices, somewhere in the darkness.

'Ahh!' said Armitage. 'A couple of you seem to

actually be awake. Is anyone else ready?'

A few more voices responded this time.

'Perhaps I should ask one more time,' said Armitage. 'My question was, ARE . . .' (*whipcrack!*) '. . . YOU . . .' (*whipcrack, twirl, somersault, double whipcrack!*) '. . . READY?'

'YESSSSS!' screamed Hannah, at the top of her voice, and Granny, and every single other person in the Big Top.

Armitage rested one hand on his hip, and slowly, critically, began to stroke his chin. 'Mmmm,' he said. 'Sounds like we sold maybe half the tickets this evening. That's a shame. I do so hate a flat atmosphere. Maybe I should ask one last time. Are you . . . those of you who happen to be awake . . . and I do so hate to repeat myself . . . but would you mind terribly if I just checked . . . are any of you . . . by any chance . . . ready?'

'YEEEESSSSSS!!!!'

The sound was deafening. Hannah had never made so much noise in her life. Granny shouted so loud, her false teeth fell out of her mouth and onto her lap. Every single person in the tent had given that 'yes' everything they had, and more, with cherries on top and whipped cream and chocolate sprinkles.

'Oh,' said Armitage, as if mildly surprised. 'That's good. But ready for what?'

Silence fell. Softly, a drum roll began.

'Are you ready, by any chance, to be amazed?'

Armitage began to pace the perimeter of the ring, which was now fully illuminated, doing an unusual prancey walk of enormous strides with each step crossing over the path of the previous one.

'Are you ready to be thrilled? Are you ready to be astonished and astounded, stunned, startled, surprised, staggered and stupefied? Amused and confused? Are you ready to be delighted and excited? Wooed and wowed? Titillated and titivated, teased and tricked? Are you? Well, are you?'

'YEEEESSSSSS!!!!'

'Good. Because that means we are all in the right place. And so . . . ' (*whipcrack*) ' . . . with no further ado . . .' (*whipcrack, cartwheel, somersault, spin, whipcrack whipcrack whipcrack*) ' . . . I bring to you . . . the incredible . . . the devastating . . . the quite spectacularly splendiferous . . . Maaauuuurrrrrrrrrrrrrice and Irrrrrrrrrrrrrrrrrrrrrrrrrrrrrrrrrrena!'

EIGHT

The burglarising begins

ARMITAGE PRANCED OFF STAGE, and as he did so, Maurice pranced on, exhibiting such a prancey prance that everyone in the audience immediately revised everything they thought they knew about prancing. Armitage's prance, they now realised, was barely a prance at all. *This* was a prance.*

Irrrrena followed closely behind, her body rippling and swaying, glistening and twinkling with body oil. Her mouth was pulled into the kind

---

*This paragraph breaks the world record for the highest number of uses of the word 'prance', previously held by the first paragraph of *A Prancer's Guide to Prancing* by Peter Prettyfoot.

of smile you might get if you attached opposite corners of your top lip to clothes pegs, strung each peg on a piece of string, then pulled outwards as hard as you can. Irrrrena wasn't very good at smiling. Her expression was the kind of thing that went less well with a thought such as, 'Hello, it's lovely to be here,' than with something along the lines of 'Oh, my God, that shark's about to bite my leg off!'

However much she practiced in the mirror, Irrrrena's smiles always just looked startled rather than happy. But at least she tried. Maurice didn't approve of smiling, and never even attempted it. The closest he came was a small curl to one corner of his mouth, which generally just meant, 'Yes, I really am as amazing as I look.'

Maurice uber-pranced to a purple velvet rope that had now appeared in the middle of the ring, dangling down from the top of the Top. He climbed

it quickly and easily, using just his arms. His legs stuck out straight in front of him, and the left hand corner of his mouth curled slightly upward, meaning, 'Yes, I really am climbing this rope without using my legs.'

Irrrrena followed, also without using her legs, but with a slightly different smile, which seemed to mean, 'I'm trying to make this look easy but IT KILLS!'

Once they were up on their trapezes, they began to do the jazzy stuff that trapeze people do, swinging and flinging, swirling and twirling, crossing and tossing, somersaulting and eating cakes. (One of those is a lie. Just checking your concentration.)

Meanwhile, Jesse was crowbarring open the dining room window at 17 Scunge Crescent. He did a swift circuit of the house, grabbing money, jewellery, a laptop, two credit cards and a tin of sardines. Jesse liked sardines. In Jesse's opinion, sardines were the chocolate buttons of the ocean. You may disagree, but since this is not a book about seafood, perhaps we should focus on the more important point, which is that he was burglarizing 17 Scunge Crescent, nicking everything small and valuable (or sardiney). Jesse didn't like stealing –

he truly hated the idea of taking things that didn't belong to him – but it was not possible to keep a place in Armitage Shank's circus without playing a part in his dastardly plans, and without this job, Jesse had no possibility of finding another one. There isn't much call for neurotic, allergic, shy, vertigo-afflicted human cannonballs. Without this job, he'd have nothing to do, nowhere to live, no money, and nothing to eat (apart from this one tin of sardines).

Jesse hated himself for stealing, but he also hated himself for being neurotic, and shy, and itchy, and having vertigo, and for being a human cannonball when human cannonballing was his least favourite activity. Jesse suffered from what you might call low self-esteem. If you ever meet Jesse, please be nice to him, unless he is robbing you at the time, in which case – be mean.

'I wish I was a zoo keeper,' he muttered to himself, as he finished his circuit of the house, shoving a last handful of valuables into his pocket, 'or a deep sea diver, or astronomer, or speleologist. I don't even know what a speleologist🕷 is, but I know it would be better than this.'

He slipped out of the window, pushed it back into place, and ran to the Big Top, carrying a baggy brown bulging bag of burgled booty.

By the time he got back to the tent, Hank and Frank were already on stage. Hank was carrying a ladder, Frank was standing in front of a paddling pool, next to another stepladder, on which was balanced an open tin of paint. He was trying to choose whether to eat a banana or a custard tart. He asked the audience's opinion, and everyone shouted, but with no conclusive decision. Frank decided to put the custard tart up

---

🕷 A speleologist is somebody who explores caves. Jesse, by the way, was also a claustrophobic, which is somebody who hates confined spaces, so he would have hated being speleologist almost as much as being a human cannonball, but he still would have preferred it to being a thief.

high, next to the tin of paint, and to eat the banana, which he peeled slowly, tossing the banana skin aside. It landed just in front of where Hank was taking his ladder.

'HANK!' yelled Frank. 'Watch out!'

Hank stopped dead, moments before his foot planted itself on top of the banana skin, and turned round. His ladder swung, almost whacking Frank in the head, but just in time, Frank ducked and stood up again.

'What?' said Hank.

'I said watch out for the banana skin.'

'Oh,' said Hank, turning round again, swinging his ladder and bashing it into Frank's ladder, which was now holding a tin of paint and a custard tart. The ladder wobbled, but Frank leapt forward and steadied it, just as Hank said, 'What banana skin?' and swung his ladder once again, causing Frank to leap back from the just-saved custard tart and tin of paint and duck down as the ladder swooshed centimetres above his head.

'Over there,' said Frank.

'Where?' said Hank, swinging his ladder. Frank ducked, stood, told him to be careful, ducked again as he turned back round, then ducked yet again as he swung once more in response to his warning that Hank's shoelace was undone.

This was Billy's favourite moment, as he waited in the wings with Narcissus, listening to the audience laughing and laughing, waves of mirth crashing towards him, the sound of hundreds of people he'd never met and never would meet, having a good time. For minutes on end, Hank and Frank drew this out, a whole performance of awful accidents almost but not quite happening. Eventually, when it seemed as if the audience wouldn't be able to take it anymore, the teetering tower of near-disaster that had been hanging over them since the moment they took the stage began to topple, and in a more spectacular way than anyone had imagined, chaos swept in.

Billy listened with relish to the roars and yelps of glee plunging towards him from the audience, waiting for his cue. He heard the laughter peak, and moments later Hank ran past him, wearing nothing but a pair of red and white underpants, soaked to the skin, his face covered in custard, his back smeared with paint, his front with sawdust. Frank was close behind, wedged into a ladder, a half-broken chair jammed over his head, with his shoes on backwards and his clown-hair hanging in a dark singed lump from one side of his head. They both had the look on their faces that you see on long distance runners as they cross the finish line in last place.

'You ate the banana too fast!' snapped Hank, to Frank.

'You swung the ladder too slow!' barked Frank, to Hank.

'You threw the custard pie too far!' yapped Hank, back to Frank.

'You lit the match too close!' yelled Frank, back to Hank.

As the sound of Hank and Frank's bickering receded, Billy heard the high wail of a clarinet fill the auditorium. This was his cue – the moment his whole day built towards. He took three deep breaths for calmness, one more for concentration, then another one for luck, and rode out into the ring, with Narcissus's body swaying and lurching underneath him.

As the warmth of the spotlight hit his face, two entirely contradictory thoughts popped up in his brain. This was not a good moment to start having Thoughts, but Thoughts are like that – they are mischievous things that have a habit of turning up when you least expect them and demanding instant hospitality.

Thought One: *You can't risk being thrown out of the circus. If you didn't have this moment each day, you'd shrivel up like a plant without water, or like a camel without taramasalata.*

Thought Two: *Right is right and wrong is wrong. This evening might be your only opportunity to turn yourself into an honest person – to find your way back to being an Espadrille, not a Shank. If you don't go for it tonight, the chance might never return.*

As Billy circled the ring on Narcissus's back, building towards his first trick, Thoughts One and Two wrestled and tussled and tumbled and fought, rolling back and forth inside his skull. This was really quite distracting.

It is hard to see out beyond the glare of a spotlight, but for a brief moment, shielding his eyes using a movement disguised as a salute, Billy looked up at the seats he had given to Hannah. She was right there, perched on the edge of her chair, smiling the most wonderful smile he had ever seen. Their eyes met, Hannah gave a huge two-armed wave, and at that moment Thought Three crashed in, smashing Thoughts One and Two to pieces.

Billy had decided. Whatever the consequences, wherever Hannah's plan led him, he was in. Tonight was the night.

At this very moment, Maurice and Irrrrena finished scaling the drainpipe at Houghton

Mansions and clambered onto a narrow concrete ledge. Maurice somersaulted over a railing and pranced across the terrace (some habits are hard to break), then, with little difficulty, jimmied open the glass doors of the penthouse, the poshest apartment in the whole town.

But back to Billy. Everyone knows you can't train a camel. Well, maybe not everyone, but people who know anything about camel training know it can't be done. Narcissus, however, was unique, and not only for the accuracy with which he could spit camel goo.

Narcissus did two circuits of the ring with an expression on his face somewhere between aloof and patronising, as if to let the audience know that entertaining humans was beneath him, and only worth doing in exchange for a pre-negotiated quantity of pellets. Then, prompted by a secret signal from Billy, Narcissus pirouetted (as much as a half-ton animal with four legs, two humps and a boy on its back can be said to pirouette) and ran in the opposite direction, while Billy did a similar pirouette (as much as it is possible to pirouette while wedged between a pair of jouncing camel humps), so he was now riding backwards, going in a different direction, but facing the same way as before. This generated a ripple of applause.

Maurice and Irrrrena were meanwhile emptying the Houghton Mansions penthouse of everything valuable and portable, without even pausing to look for sardines. By the time they got back to the Big Top, carrying two huge bags of loot, Billy was at the climax of his act, standing on Narcissus, facing sideways into the ring, being trotted round in circles while firing a bow and arrow with unerring accuracy into a pile of balloons, which he was bursting one by one.

Narcissus got extremely cross if he ever heard anyone saying he'd been tamed, because he hadn't. He simply chose to co-operate, of his own free will. He was still very much his own camel, and if anyone other than Billy ever asked him to do anything, he took great pride in his unshakeable determination to remain resolutely unhelpful, independent, obstinate and, frankly, downright rude. I shall leave it up to your imagination as to what happened to anyone who tried to force Narcissus to do anything against his will. Let's just say that camel goo is involved, and nobody had ever crossed him twice.

Billy treated the audience to one final burst of on-camel knife juggling, then leapt to the ground and gave his final bow. Before turning to leave the stage, he looked upwards towards Hannah. She was on her feet, clapping and cheering. He gave a special bow just for her, then added a private nod, with a knowing glance, that Hannah understood instantly.

It was time.

NINE

We trust no-one

AS BILLY BACKFLIPPED and cartwheeled off stage, Hannah looked to her right and was pleased to see that despite the cacophony* of cheering, clapping, stamping, whistling and whooping, Granny was fast asleep. She was smiling to herself – enjoying the show in her own special way – but was in no condition to notice her granddaughter slip past her, down the aisle, and out of the Big Top. It wasn't exactly the most stealthy of departures, either, since Hannah had a

---

* I have an uncle who collects cacophones. These are Victorian machines for playing cacophonies, which used to be recorded on brass discs roughly the size of a dinner plate, and are thought to be the loudest hand-powered device ever built. A cacophone looks a bit like a half-straightened-out tuba connected to a pair of bellows, a crank and a foot pump. They are very hard to find. Even my uncle, president of the International Society of Cacophonists, only has two.

lump of half-melted candy floss stuck to the sole of her shoe, which squelched and squerched with every step, but Granny was such a heavy sleeper that a church bell, a smoke alarm and a police siren set off under her chair probably would have made no difference. Granny snored on, dreaming of candy floss clouds perched on telegraph pole sticks, and Hannah sneaked away.

She made straight for Narcissus's living quarters (woe betide? anyone who Narcissus heard calling it a cage), and greeted Billy with a big hug. She didn't even know she was going to hug him – it just happened – but Billy didn't seem to mind. Among circus folk, this kind of behaviour was probably perfectly normal. Perhaps this was why it had happened. Hannah was definitely feeling distinctly circussy, as if she somehow belonged out here, among the performers, rather than in there, with the audience. This felt like *her* place, in a way

---

? Nobody actually knows what 'woe betide' means.

that her actual place – the town where she lived, the home she shared with her parents – never did.

You know that feeling when you've had an itchy foot for hours, and you haven't been able to get to it, then you finally take off your shoe and sock and give it a good old scratch, and a wave of hot velvety gorgeousness just bursts out and rampages through your whole body? Well, imagine this happening to a centipede, and it's scratching all one hundred feet at once. That's how Hannah felt.$^{\pi}$

From where, you may wonder, did an ordinary girl born into a humdrum family (no offence), in a humdrum little town in a humdrum part of a rather humdrum little country (no offence), get this strong feeling that she belonged among circus artistes? Coincidence? Happenstance? Freak event in the tumbling together of squillions of strands of genetic material? Wonder on, bonnet-lifters. Wonder on . . .

π Mathematicians among you may be thinking that a centipede can only scratch a maximum of fifty feet at any given time, since you need one leg to scratch the other. Not so. An abrasive surface can be used.

'Ready?' said Hannah.

'Ready,' replied Billy.

While Hannah and Billy settled Narcissus, Fingers O'Boyle took to the stage. Close-up work was Fingers' true speciality, but that's not to say he didn't know how to command a Big Top. He always liked to kick off with one of the classics, so he began by striding around the ring (Fingers never pranced, and was vehemently opposed to prancing, prancers, prancists, pranotomy and prancification) carrying three metal rings which he tossed, rolled, twirled and balanced. Sometimes the rings clanged together, sometimes they passed through one another. That was all. But everyone in the auditorium was somehow mesmerised, as if he had made water flow upwards, or gravity do a loop-the-loop, which in a way he had, because it seemed to be up to Fingers O'Boyle, rather than the laws of physics, whether the rings behaved like metal or air.

It wasn't magic, of course. It was just dexterity and skill, but the dexterity was so dextrous, the skill so skilful, that the effect was, quite simply, magical.

Hank and Frank, meanwhile, had wiped off the worst of the custard and paint and sawdust and charred wig and make-up and sweat, and dressed themselves in black tracksuits. No, they weren't going to a jogger's funeral, they were going burglarising, to Privet Place. They used pretty much the same technique as their colleagues, except that they liked to start with a conversation along the lines of the following:

'You go upstairs, I'll do the downstairs.'

'No, you go upstairs and I'll do the downstairs.'

'Why should I go upstairs?'

'Why should *I* go upstairs?'

'You always go upstairs.'

'No I don't.'

'Yes you do.'

'No I don't, and why should you choose anyway.'

'Why should *you* choose?'

'Because you always choose.'

'No, I don't.'

'Yes, you do.'

'Says who?'

'Me.'

'Me who?'

'What? What do you mean?'

'You, that's who.'

'What are you talking about?'

'I'm talking about your attitude.'

'What attitude?'

'Oh, all right. *I'll* go upstairs.'

'I thought you wanted to go upstairs.'

'No, I don't.'

'Yes, you do.'

'No, I don't.'

'Just go upstairs!'

'You go upstairs.'

At this point, Princess and her prized pack of panicky puppies began to woof, yap, howl, growl, yowl, snarl and bark.

Hank and Frank went silent.

Briefly.

'You've set the dogs off!' said Hank.

'*You've* set them off!' replied Frank.

'*You* have.'

'*You* have.'

Etc.

Hank and Frank were not very good burglars. On stage, they made a precise and carefully controlled routine look like total chaos; off stage, in their criminal chores, they turned what ought to have been a carefully controlled routine into something that approached total chaos. In short, they clowned like burglars, but they burgled like clowns.

Meanwhile, back at the Big Top, Hannah and Billy were just beginning phase one of their plan.

'First things first,' said Billy. 'We need the key.'

'What key?'

'To the truck. Follow me. You're the look out.'

'Brilliant! I've always wanted to be a look out!'

Billy dashed off between a row of caravans, and

Hannah sprinted behind.

'Wait!' she whisper-shouted.

'What? We have to hurry.'

'It's just . . . what am I looking out for?'

'Armitage!'

'Oh. Right.'

'Or any of the others. We trust no one.'

'OK.'

'Except each other.'

'Of course.'

'Now let's go.'

They soon arrived at a caravan that was larger, glitzier, sleeker and generally superior in every way to all the other caravans. Apart from anything else, it was silver, like a bullet, not white, like a fridge. (Which isn't to say that bullets are better than fridges, just that silver is a much cooler colour for a caravan.) This was Armitage's caravan. Inside, a light was on.

Billy stood on tiptoes to look in through the window, but there was a problem. He wasn't tall enough. He jumped, but there was a similar problem. He couldn't jump high enough.

Hannah cupped her hands together. 'Bunk up,' she said.

'Are you strong enough?' Billy asked.

'Of course I am. I bunk people up all the time.'

He put a hand on Hannah's shoulder and raised himself up into her hand-stirrup. It was then that Hannah realised they had a third problem. Billy was heavier than Hannah's usual bunking companions, and she wasn't strong enough after all. Her fingers were slipping. Billy, meanwhile, glancing swiftly through the window, realised that there was also a fourth problem. Armitage was inside, which wasn't good, and he was COMING OUT, which was worse.

As luck would have it, problems number three

and four combined to produce their own solution.

Before Billy could indicate that he had to get down, Hannah's hands gave way. Billy fell, landing on Hannah. Hannah fell. Billy rolled under the caravan, and just as the door above him began to swing open, he reached out and pulled Hannah in after him.

They held their breath as a pair of black suede trainers descended the steps that were just inches from their noses.♥ Armitage paused, his feet holding still for a moment as if he was looking all around, then, with a strange toes-landing-first run, he dashed off into the darkness.

Billy recognised the outfit: head-to-foot skin-tight black Lycra, black leather gloves, black eye mask. This was Armitage's burglarising kit. Theatrical? Perhaps. Subtle? No. Practical? No. But Armitage was a performer through and through, and he simply couldn't undertake any task without

---

♥ To convert that into metric measurements, 'inches' here means 'centimetres'. 'Centimetres' however, is an ugly word, and makes it sound like I have got a tape measure and figured out the exact distance between the noses and feet in question, which I haven't, so I'm going to stick with 'inches'. If vagueness (or imperial measurements) annoy you, here is a suggested nose-to-foot distance: 7.3 cm.

the proper costume.

Armitage considered his attire to be a masterpiece of camouflage. He thought it made him almost invisible.

It didn't. Whenever he walked down the street wearing his black Lycra onesie, everyone noticed him, everyone stared, and many people actually burst out laughing. However, it did still work as a cunning disguise, since all the people staring at him simply thought, 'Oh, look. There's a man going to a fancy dress party dressed as a burglar.' It never occurred to anybody that he actually *was* a burglar. See? Cunning.

The sound of three hundred gasps, followed by a drum-roll, a few seconds of silence, then one or two screams, immediately drowned out by a tumultuous round of applause, burst from the Big Top, indicating that Fingers had not been eaten alive in a tank of piranhas, but had miraculously popped out of an exploding box on the other side of the stage. In other words, he'd finished his act. Billy knew Fingers would be going straight off stage, round the back, covering himself in a cape, and rushing to join Armitage at the post office. There was no time to waste.

TEN

This is where things get interesting (not that they were boring before (at least I hope not))

THE CONCEPT OF IRONY can be hard to define, but most of us know it when we see it. Here's a good example. Armitage's caravan was equipped with a burglar alarm, which he always switched on when he went out burglarising. This wasn't any old alarm, but a home-made device that played 'Yankee Doodle Dandy' at top volume from a loud-hailer on the roof if anyone other than Armitage opened the door.

Thanks to Armitage, Billy had been given an

education that was atrocious in all subjects except two: camel riding and theft. Sadly for Billy, there were no GCSEs on either of these topics. While many children imagine themselves running off to join the circus and having wild adventures, Billy dreamed of going to school and sitting exams. This is irony of a different kind. We all want what we haven't got. It's human nature.

Camel nature is different. Camels want what they have got, assuming what they've got is a bucket of taramasalata and room to doze. Most of us would be far happier if we could take a more camelistic approach to life. But enough philosophosophising.🎓 We have a set of keys to steal.

Billy was a bright lad and a keen student. This had made him an exceptionally good thief. He'd brought with him one simple tool for the task at hand: a coat hanger. He bent and twisted it into a

---

🎓 Philosophosophising is like philosophising, which is like thinking, only more so. People who are really deep sometimes philosophosophososphisticise, but only after years of training.

new shape, a long, stretched-out question mark, and said to Hannah, 'I need another bunk-up. Do you mind if I step on your head?'

In truth, she did mind, but something about Billy made it almost impossible to say no. She cupped her hands, and he instantly zipped upwards, alternating footholds between parts of her body and bits of the caravan's window frame. As it turned out, Billy managed to get up on the roof without resorting to a head-step, and gave Hannah a big grin and a thumbs-up from his high perch.

Hannah smiled back, trying not to look too obviously relieved. Billy took a penknife from his back pocket, opened a box on the roof and snipped the wires that powered the 'Yankee Doodle Dandy' alarm. The same knife then slipped neatly under the catch of the caravan's sky-light, allowing Billy to reach in with one arm – an arm that was now holding the stretched-out coat hanger.

The keys were hanging from a hook just inside the door. At first it seemed too far to reach, but with an extra-long stretch, holding his home-made grabber with the very tips of his fingers . . .

[If this was a film, there'd be a whole long drawn-out bit here where our hero almost gets the keys, then he doesn't, then he does get them, then he slips and drops them, and he seems to despair, then he thinks of some amazing new idea, and stretches a bit further, and gets them off the floor just as someone scary comes into view and almost catches him, and the clock is ticking, and the person is getting closer, and Hannah is saying, 'Now! Now! We have to leave now!' and Billy's saying, 'But I've almost got it,' and Hannah's saying 'You're crazy, we have to run for it!' and Billy's saying 'I've almost got it. You run and save yourself!', and Hannah's saying, 'No, we're a team. We're in this together!', and Billy's saying, 'Just five more seconds!',

and Hannah's saying, 'We haven't got five more seconds!' then Billy slips, and drops the keys again!!! So Hannah steps out of the shadows and distracts the random scary intervening person with a clever trick that makes him not notice the clattering, grunting, thieving that is going on RIGHT ABOVE HIS HEAD AND WE CAN HEAR IT BUT THE SCARY PERSON HASN'T NOTICED YET! The tension is unbearable. NOW HE'S HEARD THE NOISE ABOVE! Disaster is inevitable! They are DONE FOR! But Hannah convinces random scary stranger that the noise is something else coming from somewhere else and he should run off and investigate without delay. And he falls for it! And Billy gets the key! Incredible! Amazing! Spectacular! And to a soundtrack of soaring brass and sawing violins the two of them run off hand in hand with beautiful smiles on their beautiful faces showing beautiful rows of beautiful teeth. But films can be kind of cheesy, so we're not *going to do that. Besides, (between you and me) Billy's teeth were not his strong point. While he was very good at shooting a bow and arrow from the back of trotting camels, he was not so good at tooth-brushing. Or hair-brushing. Brushing of any kind, in fact, was just not one of his interests.]*

. . . where were we, again? Oh, yes. Billy, with an extra-long stretch, had just managed to lift the keys off their hook, towards the sky-light, and out.

Phase one of Hannah and Billy's plan was complete. The burglar had been burgled.

◆◇◆◇◆

Just as Billy was breaking into Armitage's caravan, Armitage was picking the lock at the post office. This took a rather more sophisticated method than Billy's penknife, but there weren't many locks that Armitage couldn't get through, and this one took him little more than a couple of minutes.

He then tiptoed in – not that anyone was likely to hear him, but he was in character, and felt that burglars ought to tiptoe – and made his way towards the safe.

☞

As this was happening, Jesse strode onto the Big Top stage, accompanied by Irrrrena, who (freed from the demands of trapeze artistry) was now oiled from head to toe in a way that made her so shiny you could have plonked her on a clifftop and used her as a lighthouse. Behind them, pulled into the ring by a bored-looking elephant, was Jesse's enormous bright red cannon.

☞

Armitage was clearing a work space in front of the safe when Fingers arrived, with a simple cape over the top of his magician's costume, carrying a black holdall. They greeted one another with a quick nod, and Fingers unzipped his bag.

Inside were two lumps of grey goo. Two lumps of very important and expensive and dangerous grey goo.

Experts in goo and experts in explosives will know what this was. Doh! I've given it away. Yes, these were two lumps of safe-cracker's explosive, which Fingers proceeded to attach very carefully to the hinges of the safe. Armitage then set up a fuse, which he connected to a wire, which was carefully unravelled as they retreated behind the nearest supporting wall. The identification of sturdy walls is an important, and often overlooked, aspect of the safe-cracker's art. Blowing up a safe is not particularly hard. Blowing up a safe without also blowing up yourself presents more of a challenge.

A watchdog, at this point, would have been barking loud enough to alert anyone within earshot. The post office, however, did not have a watchdog. It had a watchcat, Fluffypants McBain, who had dozed through the entire break-in, napping in his favourite spot, on top of the safe. Now, however, the smell of explosives woke him up. He knew immediately that something was amiss. He understood straight away that these were bad people engaged in bad things, and that it was up to him, Fluffypants McBain, to defend his territory.

On the other hand, he really was still very tired, not to mention peckish.

He looked across at the two men dressed in black, clutching a detonator linked by a wire to two lumps of goo stuck onto his bed, and concluded that prompt action was needed.

He yawned. He stretched. He washed his left ear. Then he made a plan. A cat's got to do what a cat's got to do. He was going to step up and take care of business.

Neither Armitage nor Fingers noticed the awakening of Fluffypants McBain. With the explosives primed, the fuse prepared and the detonator ready, the two of them crouched behind their carefully chosen wall and waited.

For quite some time, they did nothing.

Or what looked like nothing.

But if you followed the path of their eyes, you might have noticed that both of them were staring with intense concentration at their watches, which were perfectly synchronised, the two second hands ticking closer and closer to 8:55.

ELEVEN

Fluffypants McBain saves the day (almost)

'QUICK!' said Billy. 'It's 8:52!'

'Is it?' said Hannah.

'Yes! Run!'

She ran. They both ran. Through the line of caravans, around the Big Top, jumping over the guy ropes they had hammered in earlier that day, and up the hillside towards Armitage's lorry. Billy climbed the metal step to the high door, shoved in the key, and wrenched at the handle.

Nothing happened.

He yanked and pulled and twisted and tugged and heaved and hauled and wonked and wiggled. Still nothing.

'Try giving the key another turn,' suggested Hannah.

Billy gave the key a firm jiggle. The hinges of the door creaked. Bingo!❹

He dived in, reached out an arm, and hauled Hannah upwards. She slammed the door shut behind them.

'Right,' said Billy. 'We're not tall enough to do this the usual way, so what do you want to be in charge of? Steering or pedals?'

'Er . . . steering,' she said.

'OK.' Billy jumped down into the footwell and handed Hannah the key. 'Now put this in the ignition. When I say go, turn it and I'll pump the accelerator.'

'Got it.'

---

❹ This doesn't mean there was a group of people playing bingo inside the truck. I just means the key turned and the door swung open.

Hannah put the key in. She gripped it tight. She waited. But Billy said nothing.

'What's the hold-up?' she asked.

'We have to mask the noise. When this thing starts it sounds like 60,000 ducks having their ducklings stolen.'

'What does 60,000 ducks having their ducklings stolen sound like?'

'You're going to find out in one minute. Just wait till I say go.'

Billy, Hannah noticed, was staring at his watch, whose second hand was ticking closer and closer to 8:55.

◆◇◆◇◆

Jesse's act was reaching its highlight. He had already smashed a plank of wood with his bare hands, ripped in half a telephone directory and lifted up four members of the audience at once. Now he was climbing into his cannon, aided by a glistening, grinning, gleaming, girning Irrrena.

Jesse's mouth was smiling, but his eyes were saying, 'Oh, no! Not this! Not again! Not the cannon! Oh, why me? Why aren't I a fisherman?' It's amazing what you can say with just your eyes if you really try.👁

Irrrrrena walked to the side of the stage and returned with a flaming torch.🔥 She looked at her watch. 8:54 and thirty seconds.

◆-◇-◆-◇-◆

Hannah stared down at Billy, who was still crouching under her feet. He glanced up from his watch. 'Nearly,' he said.

◆-◇-◆-◇-◆

Fluffypants McBain sensed that there was no time to waste. This was it, the moment to make his move. He began to enact his plan, which consisted of six phases:

👁In fact, Jesse would have been miserable as a fisherman. Yup. You guessed it. Seasickness. He could catch it in a pedalo. Even a deep bath made him slightly queasy.

🔥 Literally flaming. Not as in, 'I've stubbed my flaming toe', but as in, 'the Olympics is started with a flaming torch.'

1. Yawn again.
2. Stretch again.
3. Wash that troublesome left ear one last time.
4. Hop down from the safe.
5. Amble over to the window.
6. Settle down in the cosy nook under the leaflet dispenser for a nap.

All six steps, I am pleased to report, were flawlessly executed. In this way, Fluffypants McBain did little to save the post office, but he did, at least, save his own life.

◆◇◆◇◆

Irrrrena looked at her watch one last time. 8:54 and forty-five seconds. She walked towards the fuse at the base of the cannon, which took precisely five seconds, and began the countdown. '10 . . . 9 . . . 8 . . . 7 . . .'

'6 . . . 5 . . . 4 . . .' shouted the audience.

'. . . 3 . . .' whispered Billy.

'. . . 2 . . .' muttered Armitage.

'. . . 1 . . .' cried the audience.

'GO!' said Irrrrena, as she lit the fuse.

'Go!' said Billy.

'Go!' said Armitage.

'*Zzzzzzzz*,' said Fluffpants McBain.

'I want a new job,' said Jesse.

An enormous *BOOOOOM!* filled the Big Top. Jesse flew out through the air across the ring, somersaulting slowly as he headed in the vague direction of his alarmingly small catching net. Nobody noticed that the boom of the cannon was in fact two booms, precisely synchronised with the drowned-out sound of a large and crotchety diesel engine spluttering (and quacking, weirdly) into action.

This was Armitage's burglarising masterstroke. Just as a skilful magician directs the audience's attention away from the hand which is tricking them, so the sound of Jesse's cannon was used in every town to mask the blowing up of a safe. Two bangs sound much like one bang, if they happen at the same time, and this human cannonball/safe-blasting double whammy was a technique that Armitage had invented and mastered. He was so proud of this ingenious method that it required all his self-control to stop himself showing off about it to everyone he met.

Even in his most modest moments, Armitage couldn't help but think of himself as a genius: as the Austen of audacity, the Beethoven of break-ins, the Columbus of crime, the Darwin of deviousness, the Einstein of expropriation, the Freud of fiendishness, the Galileo of gall, the Homer of house-breaking, the Isambard Kingdom Brunel of ingeniously kitted burglaries, the Jobs of jobs, the Kafka of kleptomania, the Lennon and McCartney of the light-fingered and mischievous, the Nietzsche of nicking, the Ozu of "Oh, no!", the Pele of pinching, the Queen Cleopatra of the quietly clandestine, the Rodin of robbery, the Shakespeare of shake-downs, the Tolstoy of turnovers, the Uccello of the underworld, the Vermeer of venality, the Wilde (or Wilder) of wildness, the X-ray inventor (Wilhelm Röntgen) of extraordinarily exciting extra-legal extraction, the Yeats of yobbishness, the Zola of zero-hour zip-aways.

◆◇◆◇◆

Fluffypants McBain woke up. Something was different. No, everything was different.

The post office had been blown up.

Two men were stuffing the contents of the safe into a huge bag, then running out of the door. And worst of all, despite his extensive efforts, Fluffypants McBain's left ear was dirtier than ever.

These people are all geniuses, which is a fancy way of saying they did something nobody else had thought of before, or did something familiar in a radically new way. There are four novelists, three composers, two scientists, poets, playwrights, film directors and painters; an explorer, a mathematician, a psychoanalyst, an astronomer, an engineer, a businessman, a philosopher, a footballer, a queen and a sculptor. If you want to know who did what, you can look them up. You could also ask an adult, but you might get a very long answer, with lots of complaints about who is and isn't mentioned.

He yawned. He stretched. And he began to wash.

❖◆❖◆❖

'First gear!' said Billy.

'I thought I was just doing the steering,' said Hannah, more than a little panicked. She'd never used a gearstick before.

'I can't reach! Just put it into gear.'

'Which one?'

'First!'

'Er . . .'

'Up and to the left.'

'OK. I'll try.' Hannah grabbed the long wobbly stick, moved it to the left, then shoved it upwards. Something crunched.

'I'm letting the clutch out now. Have you got the wheel?'

'The wheel? Yes, the wheel.'

Billy released the clutch with his left hand and

pressed the accelerator with his right. The engine spluttered, growled, and lurched.

'OH, MY GOD!' yelled Hannah. 'WE'RE MOVING!'

'That's the whole idea,' said Billy.

Of course it was. Of course it was. Hannah had chosen the steering mainly because it sounded like the easier of the two options (and also because she had no idea which pedal was which, and what they were used for), but now, sitting in the driver's seat of an enormous articulated lorry which was moving forwards with alarming purposefulness, she realised something that ought to have been obvious to her some time ago. Steering a lorry is serious. If you get it wrong, you crash. If you get it very wrong, you knock down a house.

Hannah gripped the wheel as tightly as she could. It shuddered in her hands. She could feel the power of the engine pulsing through her entire body.

There was a tree in front of her. If she didn't turn the wheel at the right time, in the right direction, the lorry and tree would have a noisy, dangerous and expensive meeting. With every second she thought about it, the tree got closer.

'Are you OK?' said Billy.

'No!' replied Hannah.

'Are you going where we agreed?'

'I think so.'

'Are you steering?'

'I think so.'

'Are we going to crash?'

'I'm not sure. There's a tree!'

'Go round it.'

'Round it. OK. Yes. Good idea.'

She wrenched the wheel. The lorry changed direction. It worked!

The tree glided soundlessly past the passenger window, unaware of how close it had come to being next year's firewood.

'We did it!' Hannah whooped.

'You mean we're there?'

'No, but I missed the tree.'

'Great. Well done,' said Billy, trying to sound encouraging, though his confidence in Hannah's driving had begun to waver. "Do you want second gear?"

'No! No. First is good. When I say brake, brake.'

'OK. Was that you saying it?'

'No. That was me saying what it would sound like when I do say it.'

'Oh.'

'BRAKE!'

'Now?'

'YES! BRAKEBRAKEBRAKE!'

Wedging his back against the seat, Billy jammed both feet into the brake pedal. With a loud, disapproving sigh, the truck jerked to a stop.

Hannah momentarily floated into the air, until her legs thumped into the steering wheel, and she flopped back down again.

'Are we there?' said Billy.

'Yup. Mission accomplished.'

Billy stood up and looked out of the windscreen. They were in the right place, directly in front of the big top. His face was glistening with sweat.

'I quite enjoyed that,' said Hannah.

'Well, I'm glad one of us did,' replied Billy. 'Now follow me.'

Billy opened the driver door and jumped down.

It was a long drop, but Hannah didn't want to look feeble, so she ignored the step and jumped too. While she was in mid-air, her stomach rose up, said hello to her throat, then plunged back down again as she landed. She tried to act as if the three somersaults she did after landing were deliberate, but Billy wasn't even looking. He had rushed to the back of the lorry, where he was climbing a row of curved metal rungs up onto the roof. Hannah took a moment to undizzy herself after the accidental triple somersault, then followed behind.

As soon as she was on top of the lorry, Billy beckoned her over and pointed at a large rusty clip. 'When I say, "Go!" lift this lever, and the side of the lorry will drop down. OK?'

'OK. But can it be my turn to say go?'

'Do you know when to do it?'

'Of course I do. It was my plan, remember?'

'Oh, yeah. Sorry, boss.'

'And don't call me boss.'

'Sorry not-boss.'

'And stop saying sorry.'

'Sorry.'

'Here they come!'

Billy crawled as fast as he could to a similar

looking clip at the other end of the roof. They both crouched, hiding from view, gripping the metal levers. In that position, silent and still, they waited.

TWELVE

The worst thing Armitage had ever seen

ARMITAGE, hurrying back to the Big Top for the grand finale, sensed immediately that something was up. His lorry – his baby, his best friend, his pride and joy – had moved! Nobody, but nobody, drove that truck except him. Just the thought of anyone else sitting in that seat operating those controls made his eyes squint, his toes squabble, his heart squerch, his liver squeak, his kidneys squelch and his intestines squit. He did not let other people drive his truck. Not ever. Never.

All successful criminals are both reckless and cautious. Despite the symphony of squiffy sensations rampaging through his body, Armitage sensed this was a moment for caution. If there were police around, he had to make sure he didn't bump into them, dressed in his burglarising costume, while carrying the contents of a post office safe. You don't need a law degree to understand why this would be a bad idea.💰

He dodged into a nearby thicket. In amongst a tangle of branches he located the leafiest bush and stashed the bag of swag. Lifting up armfuls of dead leaves and tossing them over the swag bag, he quickly managed to conceal the hiding place. He'd be able to come back for it as soon as the coast was clear. Nobody would find the bag here unless they were looking for it, and the only person who'd come to look for it would be Armitage.

He looked in all directions before nipping out onto the path and rushing back towards his caravan in time for the final costume change. Due to the thicket detour, he was running late . . .

💰 In fact, you don't need a law degree at all. Unless you want to be a lawyer. And who wants that?

. . . but not too late, and Armitage made it into the ring at exactly the second the spotlight span towards him. His cuffs weren't done up, and he hadn't had time to zip his fly, but he was reasonably confident that no one would notice.

He grinned at the audience, all the more grinnily for knowing that he had successfully robbed them. The evening had gone superbly, apart from the one strange fact of that re-parked lorry. Yes, in all the scramble to get ready for his final entry, he still hadn't had time to investigate. His criminal nose had given him the feeling that there weren't any police snooping around, but he had not yet accounted for the mysterious truck move. This was a puzzle, a puzzle that distracted him slightly during his closing speech. Such was his skill at audience manipulation, however, that even when carried off at only 90% brilliance, it was still rousing enough to generate two standing ovations, three encores and a woken-up granny.

Granny stared at the empty seat next to her, in disbelief. Hannah was a responsible girl. She didn't just run off. But she had just run off. She wasn't there. As the audience around her whooped and clapped, then slowly began to drift out of the auditorium, Granny stood in front of her seat, turning round and round, calling her granddaughter's name with increasing fear and desperation.

Then, through the canvas side of the tent, she heard a voice that she knew was Hannah's calling out one very clear word: 'GO!'

◆◇◆◇◆

The side of the lorry clanged downwards. The audience, now streaming past on their way home, froze. They couldn't believe their eyes. Inside the lorry was an enormous mound of stuff – valuable stuff – TVs, laptops, jewellery, DVD players, gadgets, gizmos and gee-gaws. Not just any old valuable stuff, either, but their valuable stuff. And also several tins of sardines.

Baffled at first into silence, then with noises of surprise, protest and outrage, the audience gathered round the truck staring in horror at the possessions that had been stolen from their houses while they were watching the show.

'It's all yours!' Billy called to them from the top of the lorry.

'Take it home again!' said Hannah.

◆-◇-◆-◇-◆

Armitage, who was back in his caravan, applying a layer of make-up remover, sensed that something was up. He knew well the sound of a satisfied audience trundling contentedly home, and this wasn't it. This was something else. He looked out of the window and saw . . . the worst thing he had ever seen in his entire life.

He darted out, towelling off the thick white cream as he sprinted towards the commotion. Avoiding the audience, he ran in a wide arc to the back of the lorry and scurried up the ladder onto the roof.

A chill swept over Billy and Hannah when they saw the look on Armitage's face as he appeared on top of the truck. Never had either of them seen an expression of such pure, intense, terrifying fury.

'I'm going to deal with you two later,' he hissed, fixing them each, in turn, with a stare so poisonous it was almost enough to turn the blood in their veins into a bleach and weed-killer smoothie. But only a moment after looking as if he would never smile again, Armitage strode to the edge of the lorry roof, faced the crowd below and, with enormous effort, as if his cheek muscles were in the final round of a weightlifting contest, he smiled. Not a happy smile, nor an obviously fake smile, but a smile with a hint of cringe, a smattering of apology and a sprinkling of fear.

'Ladies and gentlemen,' he announced, in a thinner, less booming voice than usual. 'Allow me to explain—'

At this point, a chorus of outrage flew up at him:

'People, people, people, please calm down,' said Armitage, patting the air in front of him as if it contained an invisible over-excited dog.

'Ladies and Gentlemen, simmer down, I beg of you. Please. All I ask is that you listen to me for one minute.'

'I HAVE ONE QUESTION!' boomed Armitage, in a voice loud enough to momentarily quieten the angry crowd. 'Just one question. Have any of you read the words on your ticket, or on the side of my truck? Have any of you noticed the name of this circus?'

'THE NAME, LADIES AND GENTLEMEN, IS SHANK'S IMPOSSIBLE CIRCUS. And so far tonight, you have seen many things that are wonderful, beautiful, awe-inspiring, improbable, extraordinary and exquisite, but until now, have you seen anything impossible? Have you?'

'You are right, ladies and gentlemen, to feel cheated and angry. Because you bought tickets to a show that promised to achieve the impossible and until now, until this very moment, I have failed you. If you were all standing there, shouting up at me, demanding your money back, I would quite understand. For you have seen nothing impossible. Until now. Until you looked into this lorry under my feet.'

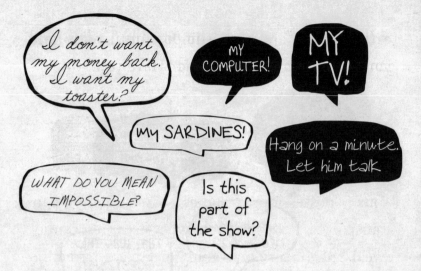

Armitage darted out a long, long finger at the end of a long, long arm and pointed down at the woman who had asked that last question. 'You, madam,' he barked, 'are an extremely savvy lady, alert to wildest possibilities of the dramatist's art. The rest of you, frankly, are more than a little behind.'

'I promised you the impossible, ladies and gentlemen, and here it is! Right in front of you!'

'Your possessions, ladies and gentlemen. Transported here, through what means I cannot reveal, but as a service to your good selves, to remind you that there are bad people about, and that your homes should be kept secure. For we at Circus Impossible think of ourselves not just as entertainers, but as public service educators, working closely with Her Majesty's police force to remind you, through the wonder of live performance, that nothing is more important than home security.'

'Think of it not just as an illusion to end all illusions, not just as the impossible made possible, but as a lesson to end all lessons. Goodnight, ladies and gentlemen. Help yourself to whatever is yours. And stay safe.'

With that, Armitage took a low, deep bow. There was a tense, sceptical silence, then one single clap at the back of the crowd, followed by another and another, until something resembling a modest round of applause trickled upwards through the air.

Armitage swivelled on his heel and turned towards Billy. 'You,' he said, 'are in big, big trouble. And you . . .' but when he spun in the other direction to address Hannah, all he saw was a pair of fingertips disappearing over the edge of the lorry, on the way down the ladder.

Armitage darted after her, jerking his body down the slippery rungs, jumping to the ground, and setting off at a run. It was not a very successful run, however, since barely had he taken two steps when a stick was thrust between his legs,

sending him crashing to the ground.

'MY COSTUME!!' he yelled, as he clambered back onto his feet. 'THAT'S A GRASS STAIN!!'

The mysterious stick, Armitage now saw, was no ordinary stick. It was a walking stick, held in the grip of a very angry-looking granny. By her side was a sleek and intelligent-looking dog.

The stick-wielding granny was approximately half Armitage's height, but the way she stared at him was quite terrifying. Had he been slightly less terrified, he would have complained to her that it was *his* job to go around giving people terrifying stares, but he was too terrified, even, for that.

'YOU LEAVE HER ALONE!' she bellowed.

Armitage didn't answer, for obvious reasons. He was too terrified.

Granny then lowered her voice into a steely whisper that was even more frightening than her bellow. She leaned towards Armitage, fixed him with a mesmerising stare, and said, 'I know who you are.'

'P . . . p . . . pardon?' he stammered.

'I know who you are. I know exactly who you are.'

'A . . . and . . . wh . . . who's that?'

'Hmmm. I'm not impressed, frankly. Not one little bit. Never was. Although you do sell excellent candy floss.'

'Th . . . thank you.'

'And let me tell you this, young man. You may get away this time, but it won't be long, now, before you meet your doom.'

'My doom?'

'Your dooooooooooooooooom.'

With those mysterious words, Granny turned and left, hobbling homewards through the crowd, the dog by her side. Armitage watched her go, transfixed by the way she moved. Despite the stick, despite the hobble, there was something graceful about her, something elegant and almost floaty, that did not look like the walk of a civilian.

By the time Armitage composed himself, the girl was long gone.

Out of the corner of his eye he noticed Billy attempting to sneak away. Keen to reassert his position as the Terrifying One, he extended an arm and grabbed Billy by the collar.

'You get back here!' he bellowed, in a voice he was ashamed to realise was an attempt to impersonate the Terrifying Granny. He coughed, trying to remember what his own voice sounded like, and said, 'Who was that girl? The one who ran away?'

'I . . . I don't know,' replied Billy. 'I think she must work for the police. She stole the lorry. I tried to stop her.'

Armitage gave Billy his are-you-lying? stare, so

Billy gave Armitage a what-do-you-mean-lying-I'm-just-an-innocent-boy-who-always-does-what-he's-told blink. Armitage gave Billy a you're-not-as-innocent-as-you-look gaze which Billy met with a but-why-on-earth-would-I-disobey-you-my-beloved-step-father? shrug.

'The police don't work like that,' snapped Armitage, giving his chin a menacing stroke. 'But I think I know who does.' He glanced at the spot where Granny had been moments earlier.

'Who?'

'She duped you. She was an infiltrator!'

'An infilwhator?'

'An infiltrator! She was sent to sabotage us!'

'Sabowhat us?'

'She was a spy! A double agent! A mole! A rat!'

'A mole *and* a rat?'

'She was working for someone, and whoever sent her knew that you were our weak point.'

'Sent? By who?'

'You don't get to my position in the entertainment industry without making a fair few enemies along the way. But I think I know whose fingerprints were on this one.'

'What do you mean?'

'I'll tell you another time. Right now we need to run for it.'

'Am I still in trouble?'

'Yes. Huge trouble. Enormous. I won't say this again. *No friends!*'

'Because they could be mole-rats?'

'Exactly. Trust no one. Except me.'

'Except you?'

'Except me.'

◆◇◆◇

That night, the circus packed up. They had two departure routines. The usual one, where they stayed the night and carefully stowed everything where it belonged the next morning, and the emergency one, where they just pulled everything down, chucked it into the trucks any old how, and scarpered before it was light. If ever there was an occasion for Plan B, this was it.

Armitage contemplated rushing back to the thicket and grabbing his bag, but considered it too risky. Someone investigating the post office break-in might still come after them, and he couldn't risk being caught with the booty.

Besides, he was a master of disguise. He could bide his time, wait until the coast was clear, then slip back into town unnoticed and retrieve the loot. That would be by far the safer option. As he drove away, through the night, Armitage contemplated his costume choices for the task. Travelling folk singer? Traffic warden? Sailor? Chimney sweep? So many options . . .

But he had to do it soon. What with wages to

pay, animals to feed, vats of baby oil to purchase and costumes to dry clean, there was not much margin for error in the finances of Shank's Impossible Circus. He needed that money.

His only fear was that he might bump into the stick-wielding granny again. There was something about her that bothered him, and not just her terrifying stare, either. He could have sworn he knew her from somewhere.

But where?

Armitage usually never felt safer, calmer, more manly, than when at the enormous wheel of his enormous lorry, but tonight the soothing effect of motorised bigness wasn't working. Ever since setting off, his pulse had been irregular, his breathing had been short, his palms clammy, and his underpants strangely uncomfortable. Why? Because like an endlessly tolling bell, one awful word had been going round and round and round and round his head. That word was dooooooooooooom!

THIRTEEN

Dawn breaks (then somebody fixes it)

THE NEXT MORNING, Hannah woke up at dawn, not because she wasn't tired, but because she was too angry to sleep. She'd been angry all night, thrashing around in bed, tormented by furious dreams about the dastardly devilry of Armitage Shank and the sad fate of Billy.

Hannah was not a wallower, a moaner or a sulker. There was no point in just lying there crossly, so she raised herself from bed, walked to the window, and looked down at her garden. Her boring garden, surrounded by a boring fence, boxed in by more boring gardens with their boring lawns and boring plants and boring patios and boring chairs. (Hannah was not a keen gardener.)

She knew she ought to just feel sorry for Billy, who right now was held captive by an evil man, stolen away from his real father, grieving for his lost mother and destined to roam the country robbing and circussing. But deep down some mad part of her couldn't help being jealous. She wanted Billy's life. Not the vanished father, dead mother, evil stepfather bit, but the rest. The circus bit. She wanted it more than she had ever wanted anything. She just *had* to have it.

Together, she and Billy had *almost* foiled Armitage and rescued Billy from his fate. Her plan had almost worked. And if a plan can almost work at the first try, then surely it ought to be worth tracking down the circus and trying again. 'If at first you don't succeed, hose yourself down, have a bite of chocolate, and give it another shot,' as the old saying goes. Or, as Hannah preferred to put it, nothing is impossible.

The circus would be far away by now, she knew that. Nobody would know where, she knew that, too.

But then, nobody else had spent long summer evenings practising tracking in the woods with Fizzer and nobody else had memorised the shape of a certain camel's footprint.

She just couldn't stay in this dull place any longer. She'd suffocate.

And the more she thought about it, the more another plan began to take shape. This plan would need an adult, but Granny was always up for a trip. Sle loved travel. She loved the way each town you visited sold different sweets. Hannah was sure she'd be able to persuade her to go. Together they'd track down Shank's Impossible Circus, and when they did, this time Hannah would come out on top. She'd free Billy and Armitage would meet his doooooom! All Hannah would need was some money to pay for the trip, because Granny was always as skint as a pocket of lint.

Hannah's whole life could change, it could begin to follow the path she knew she was destined for, if only she had that little bit of money.

◆◇◆◇◆

As you have probably noticed, Hannah's town was a sleepy little place, populated with sleepy cats and sleepy people who didn't pay much attention to their sleepy post office, so it wasn't until the morning after the circus left that anyone realised the safe had been blown up and robbed. Everyone knew immediately who had done it, but Shank and his crew were long gone, and nobody knew how to find them.

However, just as the sleepy post office staff were walking down the high street pinning up sleepily-written posters advertising a reward for any information on the whereabouts of Armitage Shank, or of the stolen money, a certain alert and unsleepy dog, Fizzer, 🐕 was taking his morning stroll.

Fizzer was in the park, checking his pee-mails, when from a distant and usually unremarkable thicket, he detected a curious waft. Something

🐕 'But who is Fizzer?!' I hear you yell, really quite annoyed now. Then, miraculously, like the sun bursting out from behind a cloud, all anger vanishes from your voice. 'Oh, I get it!' you exclaim, joyously. 'This is, like, a mystery! A puzzle! There's no answer! Fizzer is who he is. That's all there is to it. He's an enigma dog. A conundrum canine. He comes when he comes and he goes when he goes. Wow! That's so cool! This is just the best book I've ever read!'

plasticky and acrid. A hint of smoke tinged with a waft of explosive. He went to investigate.

A bag is a bag is a bag, in general. Unless it is a suitcase. But this, Fizzer knew, was something special. He could tell by the smell of it. Up close, there was a faint aroma of Fluffypants McBain and a definite honk of cash. This bag was from the post office.

Fizzer now did something extremely unusual. He began to engage in an activity which in all other circumstances he considered beneath him. He raised his head and barked.

There were many people in the park, but nobody gave him a second glance. He was just a dog, barking. What could possibly be important or interesting about that?

Only one person noticed that something was up: a girl, an alert and unsleepy girl, who was at that moment gazing boredly out of her bedroom window. This girl – and I think you know who it was – recognised the bark, and understood that if Fizzer was barking, something was up which required immediate investigation.

So she ran downstairs in her pyjamas, slipped into her wellies, and off she went. She had no idea what she might be about to find, or of the reward that was attached to it; she was just following her instincts, which were to stay alert, keep her eyes open, and never to say no to adventure.

Except that …

a few questions …

remain …

1. Will Hannah find the post office money and get the reward?
2. What will she do with it?
3. Who does Armitage suspect of sabotaging his circus?
4. Does Granny *really* know who Armitage is? Who is he?
5. Does Armitage know who Granny is? Who is she?
6. Is Billy ever going to find his real father?
7. Is Hannah going to find Billy again?
8. Why does Fluffypants McBain's never wash his right ear?
9. What is the capital of Bolivia?

All these questions will (probably) be answered in . . .